SHARP OBSIDIAN

A Novel By
Joseph Suste

CENTAUR BOOKS
Chicago

SHARP OBSIDIAN

Joseph Suste

This is a work of fiction. Names, characters, places, and incidents are the product of the author's imagination or have been used fictitiously. Any resemblance to actual persons, living or dead, events, locales or organizations is entirely coincidental.

Published by CENTAUR BOOKS
CentaurBooks.com

CENTAUR BOOKS
Chicago

imprint of Joshua Tree Publishing
JoshuaTreePublishing.com
• Chicago •

13-Digit ISBN: 978-1-941049-31-0

Book Cover Design: Paige Suste

Printed in the United States of America

Dedicated to the memory of my mother,

Agnes Francis Suste,

who believed in me and showed me how to live

with a true heart and a generous soul.

PROLOGUE

STEVEN

I never wanted a daughter—or a son for that matter. It wasn't that I didn't *want* children. I really hadn't thought about it one way or the other. Then one day—before I knew it—I found myself the father of two girls. I love them madly, but the youngest one, Julia, challenged our authority every day of her young life. In the fall of the year she turned fourteen, everything spun completely out of control.

When I looked back at that time years later, I saw the whole affair in a different light, like discovering missed innuendos in the second reading of a favorite book. Some matters that seemed important then, looked trivial in retrospect, and small concerns had lasting consequence. Personal biases revealed themselves and distortions clarified when examined from the other's point of view. That's how it happened for me and Julia, when she finally agreed to talk about it.

ANGER

A simmering pot
With a heavy lid
On a glowing red burner
On a white stove
Then
The simmer becomes a boil
And the lid lifts up, hovers over the pan
Drops down and rises again
Over and over
It doesn't stop
Until the anger is boiled away.

CHAPTER 1

J ulia exited barefoot from the passenger side of an aged, blue sedan where it idled at the bottom of the long driveway. She pushed the door shut, but it bounced back open. She slammed it hard, and it caught. Without a sign or word to the driver, she started up the gravel road, wincing with each step as stones stabbed the soles of her feet. She stopped after a few steps and wiggled into the high-heeled shoes she carried. Her ride backed down the narrow lane. The low rumble of a poorly muffled V8 faded, and a light wind dispersed the black smoke tracer that followed the car to the turn-around. When the car gained the edge of the blacktop, the tires squealed a high note that declared the intensity of the driver's displeasure, and he was gone.

Julia wobbled up the driveway on the toes of her shoes, looking for activity at the house. A terrier ran down to meet her, jumping around her feet, and wagging its tail. She stooped to pet the bouncing black fur ball.

"Hi Benjie, did you miss me?"

She smiled at the puppy and bent to pet his head. Benjamin stood on his hind legs, and she let him lick her face, then gently pushed him away. She straightened up and continued her progress up the hill with the dog following. When her attention changed from the dog to the house, her scowl returned, muddled with the remains of day-old make up. She wore a rumpled dress, and wisps of uncombed hair fluttered in a soft breeze. It was 10 o'clock in the morning.

Mary turned from a sink full of dishes at the squeak and groan of the screen door. She dropped a sponge and grabbed a hand towel as the door banged shut.

"Julia! Where have you been for two days?"

"Leave me alone," Julia said and started through the kitchen in the direction of her bedroom. She didn't look at Mary.

"I want to know where you've been. We've been worried sick about you."

Julia pushed past Mary.

"It's none of your business. I'm going to my room. Don't follow me."

Mary grabbed Julia's shoulder. "Stop right there."

Julia shook her off. "Don't touch me," she said and kept walking.

Mary followed Julia into the hall and spoke to her retreating back.

"Don't talk to me like that and don't walk away. What are you doing? You're scaring us. Nobody knew where you were, we called all your friends."

Julia stopped and turned to face Mary. "Jesus Christ, you called my friends? What gives you the right to do that? You are so embarrassing."

"When we don't hear from you, we have to do something. What's the matter, Julia, why are you acting like this, what's wrong?"

Julia stepped in to confront her mother, their faces inches apart.

"You know what? Why don't you leave me alone? There's nothing wrong except for you poking at me and getting all nosy about everything. This is why I don't come home. Just fuck off and leave me alone." Julia waved her arm to shoo Mary away and turned back toward her room.

"*You* listen to *me*," Mary said. "I have every right to know what's going on, and where you're going. You're supposed to be in school, and if I have to get the police involved, I will."

Julia laughed. "Oh yeah, well you tried that once, and it got you nowhere, so don't think you can scare me with that."

"Who do you think you are, acting like this?"

Julia hurried into her room and slammed the door. Mary tried to open it, but Julia held it closed from the other side.

"Leave me alone."

Mary pushed with her shoulder. "Open this door." It opened a crack, then slammed shut again, hard.

"No. I don't want to talk to you."

Mary backed away from the door, still facing it. Loud music burst out from inside.

"You know what? Why did you come home?" Mary shouted over the blasting music. "Why don't you go and stay gone forever? I've had it with you."

"Fine, I will. I don't need you meddling in my life anymore. I hate you."

Mary pounded the door with the open palm of her hand.

"Fine, get out of here, the sooner the better. It's way better around here when you're gone."

"I can't hear you—go away."

INTERLUDE

STEVEN

The morning of the season's first frost, I stumbled on a reminder of my daughter's crisis. We could see our breath in the house, when my wife, Mary, handed me a steaming cup of coffee and asked me to bring in some firewood for the cast iron stove in the living room. I pulled on a jacket and headed out to cut up the dead oak leaning against the fence at the bottom of the pasture.

I searched the barn for my chainsaw and found it way back in a corner, sitting on top of a white cardboard box. The lid sagged under the weight of the saw. I could still read the heavy black letters I'd written on the box lid. They declared through an oily stain: "Julia, Desert, Notes and Stuff." The words brought back memories of the trauma that consumed our family ten years earlier. Life was still unsettled when I dropped the box there, right after Julia returned.

A mud-coated wasp nest clung to the edge of the corrugated cardboard lid. I knocked it loose with a broom handle, crushed it under my boot, wiped off the dust and webs with a flannel rag, and carried the box up the drive to the house. I rang Julia's phone.

"Hello."

"Jules, guess what I found in the barn."

"God, Dad, why are you calling me so early? Thanks for waking me up."

I always forget that Julia's morning schedule doesn't mesh with mine. She'd grown out of her teens, but she hadn't shaken her habit of starting the day as late as she could.

"Sorry. Go back to sleep and call me when you've had your coffee."

"Well, I'm awake now. What is it?"

"I found a box of your stuff in the barn."

"What kind of stuff?"

"From when we sent you away to the wilderness school."

Silence.

"Still there?"

"I'm here."

"Well?"

"What would I want with that stuff? Throw it out," she said.

"Don't you want to see what's in it?"

"No, I want to forget the whole thing. Throw it out, and please, leave me alone about all that."

"I'll hold it until the next time you come over."

"Whatever."

"Sorry I woke you."

"Good bye," she said and hung up.

That's when Mary called to me from the other room.

"How's it going with the firewood?"

"Fine." I said and hurried back to the barn to get the saw.

***

Three days later, holding the box in front of me like a delivery boy, I stood at the door to Julia's apartment and rang the bell.

Julia opened the door with a smile when she saw me, but her freckled face narrowed to a pout at the sight of the box. She wore a robe, and a terry towel wrapped around her hair swami-like. The air around her felt steamy damp and smelled of soap.

"Is that the box you called me about? What are you doing, Dad? Stalking me with the evidence of my deviant past?"

"I thought we could go through this stuff, and you might tell me a little about how you felt about it."

Julia stepped back, bent over at the waist with a theatrical flourish, swung the door wide open, and motioned for me to enter.

"Come in, Dad. I guess you won't leave me alone about this until I look in the damn box." Her sigh told me a lot about the challenge I faced.

"Give me half an hour, that's all I ask."

I carried the box into the room and set it down on a low coffee table in front of her couch. Julia disappeared into her bedroom, then returned dressed in jeans and a t-shirt, the towel-turban still wrapped her hair. She pulled a tasseled cord to open the drapes, and the morning sun lit up the room.

I reached for her hand and pulled her down beside me on the sofa. She frowned at me for show, but I felt confident she'd humor her father for a little while.

I cut the hard-yellow packing tape from the lid with my penknife and pulled off the top.

"Look Jules, a mouse nested in here."

Julia shrank farther back into the couch, folded her knees up to her chin, and pulled a pillow around in front of her, "I hope the mouse is gone."

I had to laugh. A small pile of shredded paper filled one corner next to a hole in the side.

"No mouse, only the nest."

Julia looked in the box and took out an oversize blue-enamel-coated cup.

"I used this everyday on the trail. I ate a lot of crappy food out of this cup," she said, and turned it over in her hands. I watched her examine the cup, as if to confirm it was the real thing. "Everybody had one of these in their pack. We used it as a drinking cup, a bowl to eat from, and a cooking pot all in one." She looked up at me. "Why in the world did you keep this?"

"I didn't choose to keep it," I said. "But when you came back from the wilderness, you abandoned all your gear, and I threw it in this box because I didn't know what else to do with it. Then I forgot about it until I found it in the barn the other day. I thought you might want the stuff, you know, kind of nostalgic."

"Boy, you really don't get it, do you? I lived through a horrible experience. I have no desire to relive it for your entertainment or my nostalgia."

"But don't you see any value in talking this over?"

"No, I don't, so let's get this over with," she said and turned back to the box.

I pulled out a spiral-bound stenographer-style notebook, the cover smudged with dirt, the pages tattered.

"That's my journal," Julia said, her voice matter of fact, accentuating her boredom. "They forced us to make an entry every night."

I flipped through the pages. "Looks like a history of your trek. It's all dated and tells where you were, and what you were doing. There's a poem for each day. Did you write these? Here's one:

> Long black veil
> Like wind-blown sail
> Breath slows my pain
> Cooling drops of misty rain
> One emotion, then another
> Gossamer strokes and
> Soft whispers
> Caress my hair
> And dry my tears
> And then I'm gone
> All that's left is that
> Sweet gentle song

"I don't remember writing that," Julia said. "But they did try to get us to write a poem in our journal every day. Sometimes I did."

"The journal starts on the day we enrolled you in the wilderness school."

"Enrolled me? Is that what you call it? Oh no, Dad, you had me incarcerated. Only the chains and ankle bracelets were missing from our little group of inmates."

"Oh come on, Julia. It couldn't have been that bad. Don't you think you're exaggerating a little?"

Her eyes rolled up to the ceiling. "What else is in there? Let's get this over with," she said and turned back to the box.

I examined a carved piece of wood with a scoop at one end.

"What's this?" I handed it to Julia.

"A spoon, Dad. Isn't that obvious? We didn't have silverware and fine china, you know." She tossed it back in the box.

A binder clip held a stack of papers; some of them ragged where the mouse had chewed. They were letters Julia had written to me and Mary and Julia's sister, Bree.

"You kept all the letters?" Julia said. "I can't believe you kept all the letters."

"What in this canvas package?" I asked and pulled out a bundle tied with string. A sharp, black point poked out through a hole it had punctured at one end of the wrap.

"Don't touch that, Dad," she said and took it from me. I let her have it. She examined the bundle like she did the cup, untied the string, set it on the table, and unrolled the canvas. The black rock inside had a triangle shape with a short base and a long pointed apex, like a dagger blade with no hilt. One of the long sides looked about a quarter inch thick, tapering in cross-section to the other long edge which appeared dangerously sharp, so thin it faded from translucent to transparent with a purplish hue. The blade curved in a perfect shallow arc without a nick.

For a moment, I felt she'd left me, her thoughts somewhere else. I watched her face soften as she re-wrapped the black glass, set it back in the box, put the lid back on and turn to me, her eyes shining.

"How could you? How could you do that to me?" Her voice cracked, and I thought she might cry. Then she gathered herself up, turned her back to me and crossed her arms. "OK, I looked in the box. Will you take it and go now?"

A poignant quality in my daughter's speech admonished me. Her stark reprimand left me wounded. Without rebuttal, I picked up the box and carried it to the door. When I turned to say goodbye, she still stood with her back to me. I left without a word.

***

Julia invited me to lunch the next week. When she showed up ten minutes late, I smiled with relief that she wasn't going to stand me up.

"Sorry about the other day," she started. "I shouldn't have been so rude, but I wasn't prepared to look at that stuff. You made me uncomfortable, Dad. I couldn't deal with it right then. I needed time to think."

"Yeah, I shouldn't have put you on the spot," I said. "Try to understand. I've thought about this for a long time. We couldn't discuss it right after it happened, and even now, you won't talk to me about it. I didn't know how else to approach you."

"How can I get *you* to understand it was an awful experience for me?"

"Oh come on."

"It was."

"It might help if we talk about it."

"I don't want to talk about it. I don't want to think about it. You want me to admit my mistakes, Dad? Is that it? Mutter *mea culpa*, ask forgiveness? I don't want to apologize for anything. If you want me to tell you I was wrong, forget it. I won't do it. Why can't we let it go and agree it's all behind us? Why dig up an unpleasant past? I don't want to help you humiliate me. I know I did some stupid stuff. Why rub my nose in it now? It's all long ago and best forgotten. What do you want from me?"

Good question, I thought. Why is this so important to me?

"It's unfinished business, Julia. We weren't able to have an honest discussion about it back then. We all suffered, but time has healed us. There are scars, but we should be able to talk about it now. I don't know, maybe I still feel guilty about it. We're different because of it, you and me. I don't think you realize we're closer because of what we went through. We won't have finished it right if we don't re-look at it. Those who ignore history are bound to repeat it."

"Jesus Christ, Dad, that's bullshit. I'm not going to do any of the things I did at fourteen. Get real."

We realized we were too loud and attracting the attention of people at the next table. I lowered my voice. "Look, I know I'm asking a lot of you. I'm asking you to disclose private stuff that is embarrassing. It will take courage. I know you have it. I'm asking."

"Get specific, Dad. What do you want me to do?"

"I started to write about this Julia. I want your permission to use all of the material in the box: the letters, the journal, everything. I want to write the story—you write your view, and I'll write mine. The writing will give us a chance to re-examine our motives and actions. Reading each other's take on it might help us understand what happened back then."

Julia toyed with her food, stared out the window at the November gloom, then turned back to me.

"I need to think about it."

"Take this. It's a rough draft of my first three chapters. It might help you decide," I said and handed her an envelope with the pages. She accepted the envelope and looked inside.

"You've been busy."

"I promise to treat all comments with serious concern for your sensitivities and feelings."

"Thanks for lunch, Dad." She got up from the table, pulled on her coat, and tucked the envelope under her arm. "I'll call you next week."

I hoped she would read the chapters with an open mind. She stopped at the door and looked back. She blew me a kiss—a small compensation for sticking me with the check.

CHAPTER 2

STEVEN

I woke up alone in our king size bed. It was 3 a.m. I grabbed a robe, stepped out barefoot, and found Mary in our dark living room, seated at the picture window. My toes curled in an involuntary attempt to avoid contact with the cold oak planks.

"I couldn't sleep," she said to my reflection in the glass. It was almost a whisper. She looked small and vulnerable sitting on her legs in the big overstuffed chair. One of my mother's handmade quilts was wrapped around her. Her pale face and wavy red hair showed out the top. Her terrier's black nose poked out the bottom. I could tell she'd been crying.

I stooped to open the fire door on the woodstove and wrinkled my nose at a puff of escaping smoke. A couple of thrusts with the poker uncovered a few live coals. I threw a piece of quarter split madrone on top of the red glow and closed the door. Soon an orange flame lit the firebox. The crackle-spit from well-dried wood promised to chase the chill from the room. I stood up behind Mary's chair, squeezed her shoulders with both hands, and looked out the window over the top of her head. A jolly-looking, round-faced-moon-man peeked in the window at us from high over the west horizon and lit the track that climbs the hill to our country house. His cheery visage lightened my spirit for a quick second.

"She's not coming home tonight," I said and switched on the floor lamp next to Mary's chair.

"I know, but I still hope. I couldn't stare at the ceiling any longer, wondering where she is, if she's safe. What if something's happened to her? What if she came and saw the house dark and left again?"

She turned her face from my reflection in the window to look up at me, a plea for reassurance.

"She's not coming. Give me a minute; I'll make us some tea before we go back to bed. She'll be OK," I said and walked off to the kitchen.

This was the third time we'd gone through this. Each time it got harder to bear. The last time, Mary called everyone Julia knew. After she spent hours on the phone, one concerned girl friend told her where to find Julia. We called the police to pick her up from a house in town. That's how desperate we were, calling the police to pick up our own daughter. Julia convinced the cop to drop her at a women's shelter. God knows what she told that sergeant about us to get out of coming home. She would rather go to a shelter than come home? You'd think we were monsters. In half an hour, she found out they couldn't keep her against her will; a women's shelter is not a jail. She went right back on the street, probably to the same party house for all we know. We felt like nobody understood our side. This time we'd conceded defeat. We hadn't admitted it to each other, but Julia had prevailed. We didn't even try to find her. We waited—demoralized. I heard Mary calling to me from the other room as I put the teapot on to boil.

"Remember when she was little, so tiny and clumsy?"

"How can I forget," I called back. "She spilled her milk at every meal. It always ran across the table, as if by some homing instinct, to drip over the edge onto my pants."

I returned to the woodstove, closed the fire door all the way, and adjusted the flue. A raging red inferno calmed to a lazy yellow glow.

"And the time when Bree spilled hers, and Julia got so excited, 'Look, Mom, somebody spilled their milk, and it wasn't me.' We were all so carefree then. I want my little Julia back."

I dropped into the window seat facing Mary. The flashback perked her up. She smiled when another thought came to her.

"Hey, she didn't always act so sweet," I reminded her. "What about that morning you served cornflakes, and she wanted oatmeal. I'll never forget the sight of you dumping the cereal bowl over her head, milk and all. We've had better days."

"Oh, and the morning she acted up with Bree, and I asked her to quiet down," Mary recalled. "I told her 'I'm in a bad mood, Julia, you know what a bad mood is, don't you?' and she said, 'Yes mother, it means you woke up mad and you're gonna get madder.'"

Our laughter relieved the tension for a moment, but the joy faded. We sat alone with our thoughts while we gazed out at the sinking moon.

"What went wrong?" Mary asked.

"I wish I knew."

The teapot whistled for me. I went to the kitchen and returned with the chamomile.

"Be careful, it's hot."

Mary unwound her hands and arms from the quilt to take the cup. The familiar smell made her even more wistful.

"Remember Julia and Bree together on stage at the school talent show, dancing and lip-syncing to their bubble gum music. They were so cute together. They spent hours together on that performance. Now she ignores her sister. She isn't the same person anymore. All we do is fight. Every single thing is a fight, and you don't help."

"I'd make it worse if I weighed in," I said and stood up at the window looking out.

Anytime Mary confronted her, Julia sucked her right in to an emotional battle, and Mary, instead of playing the adult role—calm, matter-of-fact, stick to the subject—let Julia manipulate her into a scrappy fight. I refused to participate on those terms. It always made Mary mad— and divided—our daughter had conquered us.

"You escape to the other room as soon as the yelling starts. I need you to back me up. You need to give her some discipline." Mary wanted help I couldn't give. Discipline takes patience, consistency and commitment by both of us. Mary didn't have it in her to work that way.

"Once you two start going at each other, there's no salvaging it," I said. "You both go off on personal attack tangents. Believe me, I don't enjoy listening to shouts and screams from the other room. I can hear everything. You both get nasty. It makes me sad I can't help. Yes, I could get in there and mix it up with the two of you, but it wouldn't do any good. In a way, if I did, she'd win. It would bring me down in her eyes. It's better I stay out of those fights."

"But she might listen to you."

"No, Mary, it would only make it worse if she sensed a two-against-one situation. I tried to talk to her last weekend when you were shopping.

She pulled the same stuff on me. 'You don't understand, you're too old to get it. I can take care of it.' When I didn't give in to her and demanded answers, she stormed out the door and started walking down the driveway. We must have looked ridiculous. I followed her in the car a mile down the road before she gave up, got in, and let me bring her back home. 'Don't talk to me,' she said. I let it go at that point, but bottom line, we ended up right back where we started. No answers, nothing resolved."

"Oh, you never told me about that."

I blew on my tea and took a careful sip.

"She won't listen to me any better than she'll listen to you. It's more of a mother-daughter thing. You're closer to Julia and Bree in ways a father can never be. It's OK, I'm not complaining or disappointed. It's natural. I'm only saying your mother-daughter relationship allows you to speak your minds and throw around hurtful words and be at total war with each other, until you've talked yourselves out. In the end, after the fires have burned down, you give each other a hug and a kiss, and life goes on as if it never happened. I've seen it over and over again. It amazes me you always end up OK. You know what, Mary? She does love you."

"I know she does. It's all hormones and growing up. I know this, but it doesn't make it any easier. She gets me so mad. I can't help it. I say things I shouldn't. I worry about her safety."

"Do you think it's drugs? I mean her behavior? I wouldn't be able to tell a drug-induced personality change from her monthly angst," I said.

Mary's terrier wiggled out from under the blanket, jumped down, and scratched at the door. I got up and let him out. A cold rush of air slid in over my bare feet.

"I don't think it's drugs, but it's so hard to tell," Mary said. "She gets on the bus in the morning and goes somewhere, but it's not school. Where do you think she's going?"

"Are her girlfriends going to school?" I asked.

"Yes. I spoke to their mothers; they're all there. She's the only one. I can't even take comfort that she's with her friends. I don't know who she's with. They don't know who she's with—or they're not telling."

"Maybe Bree can help us find out," I suggested.

"No, let's not do that to Bree. She'd tell us if she knew, but it isn't her responsibility to keep track of her sister. I don't want to lay so much on her. She's asked around, but nobody's talking. I called Julia's best friend, Maggie. She claims she has no idea. She said she's tried to convince her to go to school, but Julia won't listen to her either. Maggie is worried about her too."

It was getting frosty outside. It didn't take Mary's terrier long to come scratching at the door. The dog ran in dragging a cold cloud and jumped up on the chair. Mary tucked him in under the comforter.

"I didn't tell you about the meeting I had at the high school, did I?" I asked.

"No."

"I met with the principal, her math teacher, and her English teacher. They said she refused to do the work, and skipped most of the classes. They had worthy students who deserved to be in the honors program. They were booting her out. I had a feeling they'd gotten together and made up their minds well before the meeting."

"What did you do?" Mary asked.

"Julia was there. She looked at me all smug like she expected me to put the teachers in their place. I couldn't. We had no ground to stand on. I couldn't do anything for her. You know, Mary, it's times like that when I realize Julia doesn't understand the consequences of her actions. That's what worries me."

"Couldn't you at least ask for another chance?"

"No, the time for that has come and gone. I felt like such a traitor. Julia took it pretty hard when she realized I wasn't going to bully them. Sometimes I think she's not ready for high school. Maybe she feels it too, and she's trying to compensate. She acts like she's above all that when the truth is, she's not ready."

"Couldn't you at least stand up for her?"

"With what? If she won't attend classes and won't do the work, what could I do?"

"Well I wasn't a very good student, and I skipped a lot of classes at her age."

"Did you stay out all night or leave home for days, quit attending classes altogether, refuse to do homework, and keep your parents up in the middle of the night?"

"No, they would have killed me."

I knew this was the right time to tell Mary what I'd been working on.

"You know, Mary, I was planning to talk to you about something. I've been researching a wilderness program for teenagers. I can't think of anything else to do."

"I can't stand this anymore, we have to do something, it's hard on Bree too," she said.

"Well, I've spoken to their staff about it and called some parents of kids who have been in the program. It's an outdoor experience. All outdoors. They hike and camp in the high desert southeast of Bend. They learn some survival stuff, and they have trained counselors to watch over them. It's rugged, but we have to get her away from whoever she's hanging around with—get her out from under their spell."

"Julia isn't the camping type," Mary said. "Don't you think it might be too hard for her?"

"This is too hard for us. I think it's her turn to be faced with a challenge. I've researched it enough, and I'm comfortable it will be safe. These people are trained for this, and there's a degreed psychologist to help her."

"At least we'd know where she is all the time. Let's do it, Steven."

Mary came right onboard. She surprised me with her quick agreement. She appeared as desperate as me. With a small improvement in my spirit, I felt for the first time in months, we had a plan to take the initiative.

"I'll make the arrangements in the morning. Maybe we've been too easy on her. I don't know, I'm tired. Can we go back to bed now?"

"OK, I hope I can fall asleep," she said.

***

The moon had dipped low enough to shine bright in the bedroom window, so we closed the blinds to shield us. I held Mary close, my body warmth soothed her, and I soon felt the slow regular breathing that comes with sleep. I lay awake listening to the night sounds: an owl's melancholy "*hoohoo*" in the big redwood by the porch and the disturbing staccato yelps of a coyote pack celebrating a kill. A few more restless hours of darkness passed while I dozed in and out, scared and worried, waiting for the dawn, hoping things would get better.

CHAPTER 3

STEVEN

We drove north on Crater Lake highway, fifteen minutes out of Medford, headed for Bend, a high desert city on the Deschutes River. Mary fidgeted beside me in the passenger seat. We'd conned Julia into going to a family counseling session. She's agreed when we told her she could tell her side of the story, but we hadn't told her where we were going. When she realized we were headed out of town, she exploded.

"Couldn't you liars find a head-shrinker that isn't so fucking far away?" Julia screamed from the rear seat of our old red Volvo. She added a kick to the back of my seat.

She'd ridden in silence before this. She wore her hard shell, her means of keeping us out of her new life. I didn't know how to break through. She'd made it clear she didn't want or need anything from us. I felt she hid her real purpose, avoiding the need to explain herself, because, if forced to try, she wouldn't be able to. I suspected she knew it.

Our attempts to open a crack in the shell always sent her into a rage. The hysterics worked. Any question got the same response, "none of your business," accompanied by a shrieking diversion that made discussion impossible. She'd become expert at this tactic. She used offense as an effective defense. We'd given up trying, rather than suffer the inevitable consequences of engaging her.

We didn't know what she did, where she went or why. Her answer to any expression of concern repeated the same litany: "Don't worry about it. I know what I'm doing." That last part, "I know what I'm doing," scared me, because I doubted she had thought about the results of her actions or the motivation of the people she ran with.

"I don't know why we're going to see this guy anyway; I won't talk to him," Julia shouted at the back of my head, a bait to engage in argument. Her communication link had a one-way transmission characteristic. She broadcasted to us like a radio station sending out signals. She treated us like receiver radios that could only take in what she sent. Messages back to her were blocked. Mary and I had made a pact—we wouldn't even try to reason with Julia on this trip. We had tried many times before. We had made the effort, but it always ended the same way.

Everyone in our family and all of her friends recognized Julia's ability to argue any point *ad nauseam*, no matter how illogical. We knew the fire would grow if we began to participate. With uncertainty nagging at me, I didn't want to review the pros and cons of our decision with our teenage lawyer. The less said, the better.

When we didn't take the bait, she reverted to her dour mood and went sullen again in the back seat.

Any other time, I'd've enjoy this escape through the mountain forests along the Rogue River. The road is a smooth two-lane, winding its way along the bottom of a tree canyon. Tall pines, firs, and cedars walled the path. This passage through evergreen forest usually brought peace to my spirit. Not that day.

I suspected Mary's thoughts mirrored mine. She stayed quiet when Julia erupted, played music in the dashboard deck—classic rock and roll at high volume to discourage conversation. I knew she had to swallow hard to hold her tongue.

"The antithesis of the smooth diplomat," describes Mary's character to a T. You always know where you stand with Mary, because she'll tell you straight away. No hidden agendas. She could hold her own in a good argument too, given the opportunity and a willing opponent. That would've been Julia if we gave her the chance.

The loud music kept our ferocious beastie at bay. Not that Julia threatened serious physical harm. A fourteen-year-old girl that weighed in at under a hundred pounds did not make a very scary threat, but when wakened, she issued copious amounts of verbal invective with minor provocation, and her flailing limbs could be irritating nonetheless. She was pretty, not tall, and slender with a long-legged dancer's build. She wore a rock band logo t-shirt and blue jeans. Her long brown hair framed keen brown eyes set in a soft baby face. She was smart. We'd learned to never underestimate her ability to get her way; she was confident and practiced in her skill at getting it too. The more I thought about my back-seat cargo, the more anxious I was to get to our destination.

I ignored the speed limit on the straight-aways and downhill runs, driven to get there and have the whole thing over and done. On the uphill stretches, the under-powered four-cylinder made a heroic effort with the pedal held flat on the floor. When the needle showed a frustrating loss of speed, I dropped into second, and the little engine revved in resolve to drag the heavy wagon up the hill. Sparse traffic in the middle of the week, and a wide-open two-lane road through the trees made the driving easy—but uncertainty over the drama to come made the trip seem long and tiresome.

Tension made my back hurt, and I tried to straighten up in my seat. I stole glimpses of Julia in the rearview mirror, looking for some clue in her physical appearance that would help me solve the mystery of how to communicate with her. What is she going to do when she finds out what is really going on? How am I going to explain this to her?

A jumble of fears swamped my thoughts: episodes of panic interrupted by flashes of disappointment, resolution, and self-doubt. Depressive let downs followed fast on the tail of short adrenal rushes.

Disappointment stemmed from guilt at my failure to raise a happy, healthy, and safe child. I should have been more attentive, seen it coming, stepped in earlier, but I didn't. I asked myself how I could have controlled my daughter every minute of every hour of every day, and who would want to? Then, no excuses, I knew I had to admit to responsibility. I should have instilled the values and ideals she needed to find her own way. Now she faced trouble; it was too late for a do-over even if I knew what to do over. I didn't know what went wrong and didn't know how to fix it.

That feeling of powerlessness drove me to this extraordinary measure. I had no clear answers, but I had to do something. So, we were taking the next step: asking strangers to save our daughter.

And oh—the panic. That's like the feeling you would get if the steering-wheel came loose in your hands, the brake pedal sank to the floor, and you stared into a void beyond an approaching cliff. An exaggeration, maybe, since we did have Julia in the car, and we were on our way to a potential solution; nevertheless, a constant gut twister kept me afraid she might throw open the door and jump out, even while the Volvo sped along at seventy miles an hour. I knew she wasn't dumb enough to do it. Still, I couldn't lose the thought she might.

We passed the sign for the turn-off to Crater Lake, skirted around the north side of the extinct volcano that is Mount Mazama, and began the long, straight, downhill run on State Highway 138 to the desert side of the Cascade Range. The sharp tip of Mt. Thielsen poked up on the north horizon, a natural steeple—earth offering homage to a cosmic god.

Doubt whispered to me.

Are you doing the right thing? You haven't done so well so far, or you wouldn't be in this mess. Was this even going to help her? What if Julia would come out of this phase all by herself? Are you ever going to get her back? Are you making another mistake in a long chain of mistakes that brought you to this? Is there's a better way, easier than this?

I pushed back at the doubt. I had to do something. It's not like you can go to the back of the book and look up the right answer. God, how I hated what I was doing.

I stiffened my resolve on the rationale that Julia knew she needed help and would be grateful in the end that we were pulling her out in time.

I kept hoping Julia would fall asleep in the back like she did as a child, but I knew those days were gone. She was too wound up in her anger to let that happen.

The firs and cedars receded as we descended, exposing a scrubby pine and juniper forest. Half an hour later, the road flattened out on the sparse desert lands of the high plateau that edges the east side of the Cascades. On the desert floor we made a gas stop. I worried that Julia might try to run off. More irrational panic.

We entered the outskirts of the city of Bend and searched out our destination. I pulled up at a plain-looking warehouse in a gray industrial park with the right address stenciled on the wall next to the door. The gloomy overcast day didn't help my dismal mood, but stretching my legs after the long ride gave me a minor pleasure. Our mute trio entered a reception area where clear glass panels looked in at a couple of medium-sized offices. I knew Julia still believed we came for a family counseling session and planned to withdraw into her non-communicative capsule until it blew over.

She slouched into a chair in the hall, while Mary and I entered a utilitarian office where a large man with a full beard sat behind a massive brown metal desk. Only a telephone and an open manila file folder occupied the desktop. My first impression of this jolly-looking, grey-beard vanished the second he looked up. His steel blue eyes challenged mine with an unblinking stare over a forced smile. In the first seconds of our meeting, I felt tried, judged, and convicted—put in a class with all the other failed parents who've come to him for help. His demeanor softened when he turned to Mary and greeted her with only a little more deference. He didn't stand but sat behind the desk, leaning back in a swivel chair with an air that said, "I don't need you, but you need me, don't you?" He offered us seats on two hard metal folding chairs arranged in front of the desk. He introduced himself as George Edelman.

After he looked us over, he turned back to the file folder.

"We're here about our daughter....," I started, but he interrupted me without looking up by holding his hand at the end of his outstretched arm, palm out, fingers closed like a policemen giving a signal to stop traffic. We waited for a full minute while he read from the file without speaking, then he gave us another visual review over the top of his glasses, before he began.

"Welcome to our school. I'm sure you've read the materials and know all about us. The staff told me you've spoken with some of the references we gave you. Do you have any questions about us or the program?"

"I want to know that Julia will be safe here," Mary said. "She really is a good person, it's only that she got involved with some bad people, and they took her over."

"Believe me, this is not a new story," Edelman said. "Most of the time, separating the child from their negative influence gives them the perspective they need to see how their friends are using them. Even some of the smartest kids get trapped into dangerous social groups and can't figure out how to get free. I know you're thinking that maybe you could send her to Grandmother or her aunt in another state, but the truth is, that won't work. She'd be on the phone with her pals and scheming about her return, or even running back to them. You've made the right decision in bringing her here. We're going to break the old connections, interrupt the routine, and give her some breathing space. We'll keep her safe and healthy."

Mary squirmed in the chair next to me. I tried to avoid Edelman's lock-on eyes by focusing on the wall clock behind his head. It was three thirty-three. I watched the stutter of the slim red hand as it marked the passage of the day's long seconds.

"We're all about rules here," he continued, "discipline and rules—discipline for the kids and rules for you parents. We need a commitment from you, or we can't help you or your child." His voice sounded muddy, forced out, as if his mouth was too small for his tongue. He droned on with a prepared statement about responsibilities and teamwork.

A picture of Julia blossomed in my mind like a balloon in a cartoon frame. She could have been five or six years old, all dressed up for some holiday event in a ruffled pink dress, standing straight and tall with her shiny black shoes tight together like she might click her heels at any moment and make magic happen. She had a flawless pixie haircut and a happy smile that said she felt pretty, and everything was perfect. The vision faded when Edelman's voice rose and dragged my attention back to his speech.

"...and so you've seen the program, talked to the staff, now I have to know that I have your commitment." It was almost a growl.

"Well I don't know," I said. "How do we know this is going to help her?"

"Look, you wouldn't be here if your child," he glanced at his file, "uhh—Julia, hadn't taken charge. You've relinquished your authority, and you don't know how to get it back, do you?"

He leaned forward in his chair and looked directly at me. "It's because you," he pointed a finger at me and retracted it, "haven't given her discipline. Now she's discovered you are powerless to stop her. What we are going to do here is get you back in control. To do that, I need your participation and complete buy-in."

I vacillated; the doubt rushed back, my resolution softened, panic attacked. The finger pointing was uncalled-for. He didn't have to bully. Mary turned to look at me, then back at Edelman. She waited for me to speak. Maybe she thought I should defend myself. I hoped she wouldn't start in with some lame excuses for our poor parenting performance. I wished she'd speak up and relieve the tension. I wanted her to say, "I think we've made a mistake. We're taking Julia home now, thank you and goodbye. Let's go Steven," but she didn't. She sat in uncharacteristic silence which meant she'd given me the authority to do whatever I thought best. The weight of decision drooped my shoulders. I prayed I did the right thing. Inside I wanted to cry, a real tears-and-all cry. Only a complete loser would do this to his daughter.

"OK, here. Here's the contract," he said and slid a sheaf of papers out of the folder and waived them in the air. "You can read it word for word, or I can tell you what's in it." He laid the contract in front of me on the desk top. "You are giving us full responsibility for Julia. This is an outdoor experience. There are challenging physical activities. We provide trained counselors to manage day to day activities and therapists to help your child look at their lives, at what they have been doing, to help them see the error in their ways. No brainwashing. In the main, the psychologists are a sympathetic ear they can talk to without being judged. You'll get phone reports on Fridays from the counselors. That's it. I need your agreement. If you won't agree to these rules, we can't help you."

Mary and I had already studied the contract. We'd had phone conversations with parents of children who'd been through the program. Our minds were made up before we got there, but at game time, it looks nothing quite like practice, no matter how well you think you've prepared. For my part, I had already seen Julia taken over by her so-called "friends" and could find no way to get her back. The only choice I had left was to turn her over to these well-intentioned people. Mary was fed up with the Julia we'd brought over in the Volvo. She'd lost all patience with trying to salvage her. Mary had given up. I knew the decision was mine, and Mary would go along.

"Yes," I said. "Let's get on with it."

"We're going to drug test her here, she'll overnight under constant surveillance, and go out to the trail in the morning," Edelman declared. "Now let me have a few words with her alone, then I'll bring you back in."

Julia had been brooding in the lobby. Since we'd told her we had scheduled a counseling session, I was sure she'd prepared some offensive charges to argue her case along the lines of "they are the problem and they are ruining my life." A wasted effort, but it kept her calm and occupied. We traded places with Julia and settled into the waiting area outside the office. I felt the tension in the clamp of my jaw and realized I was grinding my teeth. Mary took my hand to give me some reassurance. I knew she felt relieved we were turning Julia over to the "fixers."

It didn't take long before Edelman summoned us back in. We had no idea what Edelman said to Julia, but she didn't act upset, so I knew he hadn't dropped the bomb.

As soon as we sat down, Julia said, "This is bullshit. Can we leave now?"

I wondered how ugly it was going to get. I started to feel sorry for Julia and tried hard to swallow my guilt. My heart seemed to be beating fast. The blood rose in my face and the back of my neck tingled with tension. I shuffled my feet for no good reason.

"Just a minute," Edelman said. He picked up the phone from its cradle, punched an intercom button, and said, "Mark and Amy, please come in."

Two athletic looking under-thirties dressed in crisp outdoor clothes entered the office from a side door and bracketed Julia's chair. I realized I was holding my breath and tried to let it out without being obvious.

"Julia, you are not leaving," Edelman said. "You are going to stay with us for a while. Please go with Mark and Amy; your parents will join you in a few minutes to say goodbye."

Julia looked at me first. Surprise and confusion marked her face. I knew that look well from her childhood, a signal to me she needed help. It included a confidence that I'd step in and save her as I always had. I ached to be that father again. I agonized over my desire to call it off. I started to get up, but Mary grabbed my arm and held me back.

When Julia realized this was not business as usual, her eyes bounced from me, to Edelman, to Mark and Amy, then back to Mary as if calculating her odds in a fight. She hadn't even considered the possibility we might wrest control from her.

It was a couple weeks ago when Julia challenged me to my face: "My friends are right, you fuckers can't do anything. I can do whatever I want, and there's no way you can stop me."

The counselors took Julia by the arms. She rose, dazed, from her chair, and they led her toward the door. She accepted that physical resistance was futile, and she was too disoriented by the surprise of it all to even speak. I breathed relief that I didn't have to watch her struggle to resist. She threw us a look over her shoulder that said, "I knew I shouldn't trust you. Well I don't give a damn and you can do whatever you want—but you can't get to me. I might go along with this for now, but you can never win. I'm going to be in control no matter what. You'll see. You'll be sorry. Go to hell." She could fit a pretty comprehensive message into one of her eye-to-eye transmissions.

I watched them escort Julia out the side door and thought to myself, "Yes we can, Jules, yes we can do something," but there was no joy in it.

When the three passed through the door, I glimpsed what appeared to be a large open warehouse-space with steel shelving. The door slammed shut with a solid finality, and my stomach hit the floor. Edelman sensed our state—I'm sure he'd seen it many times before in the eyes of other Judases like us—and offered a salve. "We'll take good care of her. Give her a few minutes with the crew, then you can say your good-byes. You're doing the right thing."

He pushed the papers across the desk and pointed to the signature lines, "Sign here, here and initial there, press hard, there's carbons." He handed me a ball point.

The rules we signed on for were simple. No phone calls with Julia. Communication by letter only. We would identify persons authorized to write to Julia. We could see all the mail, coming and going. The duration was to be a minimum of sixty days, but more likely three months. Julia would spend much of her time hiking, and making and breaking camp. She'd have the attention of a therapist to discuss her recent past and stimulate thought about her future. There'd be a physical examination to ensure that she was able to meet the challenges of living in the wilderness.

We signed the documents, and I wrote a very big check.

***

Edelman led us through double doors into a warehouse with a concrete floor. Metal shelves filled with camping supplies lined the walls. Julia stood alone in the center of the space. She wore new khakis and a machine creased green shirt that gave her the appearance of a youthful forest ranger. A brown plastic tarp lay open on the floor at her feet. Others moved back and forth between her and the shelves, placing supplies on the tarp and checking them off on a clip board.

I tried to judge her mood. She was stone faced. She glanced at us with dark eyes, then down at the floor. She didn't speak. I searched for a tear in her eye, but there was nothing soft in her look. There would be no begging for forgiveness from Julia, no plea for one-more-last-chance. She was too proud for that. She knew—and we knew—the time for that stuff was way behind us. Events had momentum.

I wished I'd prepared a speech. I had avoided picturing this moment. I wanted to explain to Julia we were doing this for her, but even the thought sounded trite. I felt anything I said would be inadequate anyway.

Our appearance interrupted the process. Mark and Amy stood close by, apparently in charge of Julia and at the ready if she were to attempt any trouble. The staff people were young and serious. They gave off an air of confidence and a genuine desire to help their new charge through this particularly rough spot.

Mary told Julia we loved her, and we'd write to her soon. It was not at all satisfying, but we knew it was better to leave quickly rather than draw it out. I knew Julia would have erupted had she not been in this unfamiliar environment with all of these strangers, not comprehending what was happening and not knowing what to expect next.

I wanted to give her a hug and let her know that it was going to be all right, but she wouldn't allow me to touch her and turned away when I made a motion to approach. I wasn't sure myself that everything was "going to be all right." Maybe this was the penalty I had to pay for my failure to be a good father. Maybe what I was doing proved I *was* a good father. Crap. It was done.

Her silence hurt. Knowing Julia, I imagined she'd wish later she'd allowed that hug, but giving it then would've been saying she understood and forgave us. She may have understood, but she was not going to forgive us easily, surely not then. Maybe at night before she fell asleep, she'd let herself agree that what we'd done was best for her.

So we left her there, aching to hug her, wanting to explain, but unable to pierce her wall. It was hard to turn my back on her, but I did. When the door closed behind us, I thought the tears would start, but I wasn't sure if they'd be mine or hers.

INTERLUDE

STEVEN

J ulia appeared unannounced a week later carrying the clipped pages of the three chapters. She stepped into my office and closed the door.

"Got a minute, Dad?"

I was surprised but happy to see her. I hit the *save* icon, left the screen, and gave her my full attention.

"What's up, Julia?"

"I read the stuff you gave me," she said. "I guess I never saw it from your side before."

I welcomed her confession. She looked tense, like her admission was difficult, but without the anger she'd displayed the last time. I had hopes.

"I'm sure I didn't understand your point of view either, Julia. That's why I want to work on this with you."

"I knew you were worried about me, but back then, I never thought what it was like for you and mom when I didn't come home. I'm sorry." Her damp eyes told me it was a genuine regret.

"Hey, it's OK. None of us are mind readers."

"Well, I never realized my actions had any impact on you and Mom and Bree. When I put myself back there, I remember feeling like you and Mom were simply there, never changing, and I had made all these big changes, but you didn't come with me or see the difference. Did you guys really get up in the middle of the night wondering where I was?"

"Yes we did. Let's go down to the conference room and talk about it. I need to get away from this phone for awhile anyway," I said.

We sat next to each other in the mahogany paneled conference room. A late afternoon sun leaked in through slatted blinds and striped the table. Julia handed me the manuscript. By the look of the dog-eared pages, I guessed she'd read through them a couple of times.

"What do you think of my reminiscence?"

"It's pretty close. You took a little license in there, but the main facts and feelings are real," Julia said. "That scene with Mom is embarrassing, but it's pretty much true."

"Can I keep it?"

"Yeah, it doesn't make me look too good, but I can't deny the facts."

"So you'll do it?" I said.

Julia turned to me, straightened up in her chair, and looked me in the eye.

"OK, I'll do it, Dad, but it's only because I trust you. It has to be like you said; you'll take out anything I don't feel comfortable with. No arguments on that, OK?"

"I promise," I said. I reached over and gave her a hug. "You won't regret it, I promise. So let's get started. What happened after we dropped you off at that warehouse in Bend?" I pulled a miniature recorder out of my pocket, punched the red record button, and set it on the table. "The whole way to Bend, I was wondering what you were thinking. So what did you think when he said you weren't going home?"

"OK, Dad, you asked for it. I'll never forget that moment. I'll tell you exactly what was going on in my head," Julia said.

A long road
A slow ride
I can't change it
I can't hide
I will travel
Head held high

CHAPTER 4

JULIA

*S*on—*of*—*a*—*bitch*. I'm standing in the middle of a goddamn warehouse dressed like a fucking boy scout, and I know I've been had.

I never should have trusted them. I never should have gotten in the car with them. I try to go half way and what do I get? Dammit. Liars.

"We're going to Bend to see a counselor." I can't believe I fell for that. I should have known it was more of their bullshit. First off, I'm not the one who needs a counselor. Like they think some stranger busybody, who doesn't know anything about me, is going to tell me what to do and how to live. *They're* the ones who need a counselor, somebody to tell them to get the hell off my back. As far as I'm concerned, they're both fucking liars.

Oh great, here they come to say good bye. Like I'm gonna even talk to them when they're doing this to me, fat chance of that. I can't stand to even look at them. I'm not about to give them anything they can use to ease their conscience. He has that, "hurts me more than it hurts you" look. She looks like she'd rather be anywhere but here. Good. I hope they both feel like shit.

My mom says, "I'm sorry we had to do this, Julia. It's for your own good. Remember we love you. We'll write you soon. Can I have a hug?"

He doesn't say anything.

I cross my arms and turn my back on them. I hear Edelman mumbling to them. The door closes, and they're gone. For a teeny, tiny, little second there, I think about yelling out, "OK, I'll do what you say, but don't leave me here," but that thought vanishes—and I make an oath to myself that I'm not going to be kissing any asses.

After they leave, I look around to try and figure out what I got myself into. The place is bare-bones. All cheap metal shelves and cement floor. Nobody talks to me. They talk to each other in low whispers. The space is so echoey the sound of their voices and their boots scraping on the concrete floor bounces off the walls. They buzz around me like I'm not even there and keep dropping stuff at my feet that has a kind of new factory smell to it. They seem to be checking me out and waiting for somebody to tell them what to do next. This must be what it feels like to get drafted into the army.

How could I be so stupid to let them trap me like this? I had a feeling something was up when they hardly said one word to me the whole trip. I should have known when they didn't grind me about missing school or staying out all night. I swear I'll never trust them again. This whole thing sucks big time.

They must be really scared to do this to me. They probably think I was going to get hooked on drugs or something. I know when to draw the line. I can take it or leave it. I'm totally in control. They always over-react like I'm getting into some serious drugs like heroin, or meth or something. I'm a goddamn vegan for Chrissake. I don't eat anything that once had a face. I take care of my body. I wouldn't put any of that drug crap in my body—well, not on a regular basis anyway. You'd think they don't know me at all after we lived together for fourteen years. I can't get why they think I can't take care of myself.

What is it with this tarp and all this camping stuff? This is so bogus. If they think they can send me to camp and straighten me out, they really don't know me at all.

They're too old to understand. Their lives are over, and they blew it. Mine is beginning, and I'm not about to repeat all their mistakes. I'm way smarter than them. I can do anything I want, and I can do it my way. My life is going to be way better than anything they can even imagine. I don't need their old-fashion bullshit boundaries. They're living their boring lives, and now they want to start ruining mine. I'm free to make my own decisions, and I don't have to answer to anyone. I know what I'm doing. Why don't they trust me?

"What size are your shoes, Julia?" the Amy woman asks. She shows me two pairs of lace-up boots.

"What are those for? I don't need boots. I've never worn combat boots in my life."

"You are going to want these, Julia. You'll be doing some walking on rough terrain. They'll save your feet. What size do you wear?"

"Sevens, I wear sevens,"

"Here, try these." She gives me the boots and a pair of wool socks.

I sit down on the tarp and put on the boots. I can't believe how fast my reality is changing. I'll get out of here and never give them a chance to mess with me again. Mike will come and get me. He told me he loves me the last night we were together. He won't let them disappear me. He's a smart guy; he'll figure something out. He'll be here in no time. He's probably tracking me down right now.

I wonder what they told Bree. "Your sister refuses to be a little robot and do everything we say, so we sent her off to Siberia." Maybe she'll tell Mike where I am. Probably not. I don't know why Bree sides with them. She's still under their thumb. Not like me. I've made my break with them. I'm not gonna take it anymore.

These boots must have a hundred holes to lace up. Haven't these people heard of Velcro? I get the boots laced up and tied. I stand up in them, and the soles are so thick I feel a couple inches taller.

These assholes won't be able to keep me. They can't watch me every minute. I'll get a chance, and when I do, I'll run like hell. I'll find Donna. She's in Bend with her boyfriend; she'll put me up. Donna's a good friend. She'll probably be living in the same trailer in the woods by the river. They'll never think of looking for me there. I can hide out until they give up looking for me, then I'll call Mike—and he'll come and get me. Maybe we'll go to Portland. I like Portland, and Mike can get a construction job anywhere. Probably better jobs in Portland anyway. That's it, I'll wait them out, wait for them to let their guard down, then I'll break out of here.

I pace back and forth in the boots. It feels like I have weights on my feet. How the hell do they expect me to walk in these things? The soles are so hard they don't even bend. Oh god! I don't deserve this.

The Edelman guy comes back and huddles with Amy and the other guy. I get a sinking feeling when I realize they're gone and really did leave me here. Edelman hands over some paperwork and leaves. I watch Amy and the guy standing together reading through the papers. I'm thinking they're probably what my parents signed to commit me. So this is what I get for wanting to have my own life?

They try to blame everything on my friends, like everybody's taking advantage of me. It really makes me mad when they do that. They always talk down to me, like I'm some kind of moron the smart kids are pushing around. I know it bothered them when we wrote all that nasty stuff on the walls in my bedroom, but it was all in fun. I tried to keep them out of there, but they saw that shit anyway. Darla was the one. I couldn't stop her from getting all whorey about it and writing that stuff. I shouldn't have let them see it. I've heard the language my dad uses when he's talking to his friends and it's pretty bad, but when we do it, he gets all high and mighty about it.

A big part of it is Darla. Dad hates Darla. He thinks Darla is the reason I'm going with Mike and having sex. Darla is my best friend. If it wasn't for her, I'd probably be a little robot like the rest of the bozos in that school. We're way ahead of them. I don't understand why they think their kid is the stupid one.

Oh, and because I'm fourteen and Mike's nineteen, they think I'm a baby that can't hold my own with the big kids. You know, I really think that's it: they think I'm a goddamn baby. They think they have to do everything for me and make all my decisions for me—and I can't be trusted with a sharp instrument. When the hell are they going to give it up? I stopped spilling my milk and skinning my knees years ago.

I'm sure it's the sex thing that put Dad over the edge. He figure's I'm out every night getting laid by "older boys" taking advantage of me. So what? I'm old enough. It's my choice, it's my body. I know how to use birth control. He probably wants me to wait until I'm eighty or something, and Mom is just as bad about asking me all these questions like it's her business to know my business. I've had it with them. I don't know why I didn't leave and stay gone. I really don't need them anymore. I don't hate them or anything. I just want them to leave me alone. Why are they always bothering me and wanting to know everything I do when it's none of their goddamn business. Now they did this to me.

Amy and this guy, Mark, come over and show me how to fold up the tarp with all the stuff in it and tie it with a rope.

"Pick it up and bring it over to that bench," he says and points to a wooden bench in the corner of the warehouse. "Amy will give you a briefing on what to expect for the next few days."

I try to pick it up, but it's so heavy and awkward I can't get it off the ground.

"Here, grab a hold of the rope ties like this and pull it up on your back," he says.

I finally get it off the ground and stumble over to the bench. You'd think they could help me, but they don't. I drop the bundle in front of the bench and sit down. Amy sits next to me and starts telling me what's next. That's when I find out I'm really in for it.

CHAPTER 5

STEVEN

Our mood was glum on the drive home. I thought to say something to make Mary feel better about it, but the words wouldn't come. I wanted to be cheerful for Mary's sake, but no matter how hard I tried to turn my mood, I couldn't do it. I felt selfish, mourning alone in my thoughts.

"Well, that wasn't so bad," I said.

"Yeah," Mary said, and the silence re-asserted itself.

My mind churned. How little and lonely Julia looked standing there when we left. How many times had I put her to bed with a hug and a kiss and a story or a lullaby? We had a routine when she was tiny. Bree taking her feet and me taking her arms. We'd swing her back and forth between us like a pendulum until we got her high enough to toss her onto the bed. One, two, THREE—and she bounced onto the comforter. She loved it, we all laughed. I longed for the return of the days when she fell asleep in my arms, knowing she had nothing to fear, knowing I was there to take care of everything.

But that day, she didn't even give us a hug or any sign she understood or forgave us for leaving her there. The stone wall was up. I knew she'd feel abandoned, but she'd be damned if she'd let anyone know it. Her intransigence would see her through the first day. She'd harden up like

the time the police picked her up. She'd be bold and brazen and silent—
thinking about how to escape and return to her friends.

The silence in the car was suffocating, so I pulled over for a break at
the Rogue River Gorge. Mary and I got out of the car and walked along
the paved path, listening to the powerful roar of the tightly channeled
river rushing through fissures in ancient volcanic rock, foaming white as
it slammed against boulders, plummeted over falls, and careened around
the turn at Farewell Bend on its way to the ocean. It was the cold, clear
snowmelt of Mount Mazama, a union of streams creating the powerful
Rogue River. Mary took my hand, and I welcomed the comfort in it.

We stepped down to a low viewing platform and gazed over the
guardrail at the watery chaos below. "We did the right thing, Steven," her
voice was tiny against the tumultuous thunder of the river. "We did the right
thing for Julia. She'll be OK, it's OK," she said. I smoked a cigarette. Mary
didn't hassle me about it. It started to drizzle, and we got back in the car.

My thoughts stayed with Julia. Underlying her brave front would be
a scared little girl in shock, not knowing what to expect, and wondering
what was going to happen next. Guilt flashed; unable to solve the problem,
I'd left her with strangers. Yet, there was relief in knowing she was safe
while we tried our best to work things out.

I remembered what happened to a friend's errant sister. I knew her as
a young teenager, a beautiful girl; she became estranged from their family,
living on the street. At the time, I asked her brother, 'Why don't you do
something for her?' He told me they'd tried, but she didn't want to be
helped. How could anyone give up the love of a caring family? Why would
they? He was resigned; she seemed to have crossed a threshold and once it
was crossed, there could be no return. I wasn't going to gamble that Julia
might cross over.

We'd separated her from the forces taking her over, replacing us as
her family and challenging us for her loyalty. They had been winning until
now. I admit there was a small satisfaction in taking this round. We could
and did do something, and no, Julia can't do whatever she wants without
consequence. We had rescued our daughter from a subtle evil. I knew—as
difficult as it was that day—it was the only good choice. Right then, I had
to deal with uncertainty and sadness. I tried to keep up my hope for a
better time to come.

We drove on quietly, lost in our thoughts. We were very much relieved
to have it over with. The miles of forested road went by unnoticed. When
we arrived home, the house felt empty.

CHAPTER 6

BREE

I remember the day it happened. They came back from Bend and told me what they'd done with my sister. They made a big deal about why they'd done it and went on about how she gave them no choice. Well, of course they had other choices. This was way outside the boundary of the usual treatment we got. They must have been way scared. I wouldn't say they're over-protective, but they did try to watchdog us and be a part of our lives—and never give up their responsibility to anyone else. Guess that didn't work too good. Julia got into trouble during school hours when they weren't around. The freedom of a freshman on an open campus was too much for her to handle.

I kinda expected something because of what happened two days before. Jules and I were sprawling on the couches watching TV after school. Julia had decided to come home that day—no one knew when she would or wouldn't be there. Dad walked through the room, and I saw his eyes zero in on Julia's bare midriff which she immediately covered by pulling her t-shirt over it. Too late. Dad and I saw what looked like a brand in the middle of her belly partially surrounding the navel. It looked like a fresh burn because it was all bleached white along the edges and raised up in lines like a thin cauliflower row. I saw the look in his eye then. His mind had snapped the image. He stood there for a moment looking at her, then dropped his head, and looked down at the tops of his shoes. He didn't say one word, he didn't look at either one of us again. He turned and left the room. I'm pretty sure that was the instant mister strong and deliberate, slow and unshakeable, decided he'd had enough. I couldn't imagine he would let it go without doing something. We'd both seen it, and we knew what we'd seen. I was waiting for something to happen, but I never imagined it was going to be this.

Until then I was the dutiful older sister. I tried not to be a squealer, but I really wanted to help because I knew Julia was in trouble. I asked her about things, but she said it was none of my business. Sometimes her friends would tell me a little bit about what was going on, but I kept quiet to protect my sources. Julia wouldn't talk to me about anything. We kinda became strangers because there was nothing more important than the weather or a TV show she would talk about. I hated that.

I felt a little left out during the time Julia was doing her runaway episodes; they'd completely focused on her, like she was their only child. I kinda understood it and enjoyed a little less attention and some extra freedom because of it, so I really didn't let it bother me too much. It was kind of a lonely time for me.

I helped a couple of times when she was gone for a few days because we all got worried and tried any way we could to find out if she was OK—if she was safe. I was the one who found out where she was the second time, when she had been gone for almost a week. We sent the police to pick her up. It was a joke. That was when Dad learned the address of the boys. That really worried me.

The day after they took her, a couple of her friends asked me where Julia was. They were casual about it the first day, then it started to get intense. They were afraid to call the house, mainly because they were afraid of my dad. They kept pestering me until I had to tell them something. I thought if I told one of them she was OK, that would be the end of it— but it wasn't. I was having enough of a time dealing with the situation for myself. I really didn't need stress from them.

I tried hard not to cave-in to the pressure, but I couldn't avoid Darla for long. I saw her coming at me across the school lawn. She walked fast on her model-thin legs that were poking out of a too short skirt. The way she leaned forward showed off the pair of boy magnets that bobbed up and down in her low cut top as she walked. No one but a blind man would believe it was Darla's face that made her popular.

She reached me right as I was about to get on the bus. She knocked the books out of my hands and got in my face.

"We're going to find out; you might as well tell us. What did your stupid parents do with Julia? I know she isn't off on her own because your sappy parents would be calling everybody in town looking for her. So where is she? I know you know. Tell me!"

I looked around for support. I didn't have any friends there. I really didn't have any real friends at this school at all. I knew I was going to have to give it up sooner or later.

"OK, Darla, I'll tell you where she is, and she's there because you and your disgusting friends put her there, and my parents aren't stupid, they're smart enough to know you are no good. You took control of Julia, and they're breaking the chain you put around her neck. Julia is in a teen recovery camp; she's going to be there for a long time; you have no way to contact her, so leave me alone and get the hell out of my face you little bitch."

"Where's the camp, Bree? Where is it? We're going to get her and bring her back. They have no right to…to…to kidnap her like this. We're going to get a lawyer. We're going to get a car and go after her. Where's the fucking camp?"

Darla grabbed both my arms at this point and was stepping all over the books and notes she'd knocked to the ground.

"What's going on here?" It was the school monitor woman hired to stop this sort of bullying.

"Oh nothing," Darla said with her most absolutely innocent smile in a sing-song voice that made me want to puke. She reached down and started picking up my books and papers, all the time casting her false smile at the monitor woman. "It was an accident. Here, Bree, let me help you pick these up. It was my fault for not looking where I was going."

"We're OK," I said. "Thanks for asking." There was no way any kid in this school was going to turn in Darla and have anything but a miserable rest of her life. The woman moved on.

Darla stopped picking up my stuff. I saw the glint of an idea flash on her face, but instead of knocking them down again, nice, sweet, understanding Darla made an appearance.

"I'm sorry Bree, I was worrying about Julia so much. We have to do something. This can't be allowed to stand. I know what you're saying, and I have to do something for Julia. I feel so guilty about it."

"No you don't, Darla. You've never felt guilty for anything in your life. You're a lying little bitch. I'm not telling you anything."

Sweet Darla folded her tent. Real Darla grabbed me again, and this time put her mouth right next to my ear and whispered, "If you don't tell me right now, I'm going to tell everyone in this school that your father has been abusing you since you were four-years- old—and you like it!"

She swung her arm down to knock the books out of my arms again, but I saw it coming and turned my body so the blow bounced off my back. I shook off her other hand and climbed up the steps into the bus as the driver was about to close the doors. This is why I hate Darla. This is why I will always hate Darla.

I turned around and looked down at her from the steps.

"Las Vegas," I said. "They sent her to Nevada, that's all I know."

The telephone lines must have been glowing red hot that night because by the next day, everybody knew. Even people who didn't know Julia, knew she had been sent away to Las Vegas for counseling. The barrage of questions from the students and teachers lasted a couple more days. I told them I didn't know anything more, and if they wanted more information, to call my dad. Of course none of them ever did, because they weren't really concerned about Julia. They were only using her as the dupe in their stupid daily drama.

It's hard to face
Once made mistakes.
Under judgmental stare
Of those who care.
 It's hard to look
My pride is took.
Unsure—
My eyes reveal the lies.

CHAPTER 7

JULIA

Well, today being my first day, I'm sorta overwhelmed. The whole thing is unreal. I really don't want to be here. I have a life that I've been plucked from and not even been told what's going on. I don't feel I need to be here. I want to leave as soon as possible, but my impression is to be positive, do what I'm told, and get out of here as soon as I can. I really miss my friends. They don't even know where I am or what happened. I didn't even get to say good-bye to Mike or Darla. The thought of sixty days minimum without seeing them kills me. I really love my friends; they are my family as much as my parents and my sister, but lately I've been closer to them. They understand me.

Everything here is so structured and exact. It kinda makes me sick actually. It really bothers me, but oh well, I figure I have to deal with it because right now, I don't really have a choice if I want out of here. I'm trying hard to think positive about it, maybe it will be a good experience, maybe it will help what everyone thinks is wrong with me. The only thing I see wrong with me is I have my own opinions and feel very strongly about them. I'm stubborn, and I don't like feeling out of control. I don't like doing things for other people that they shouldn't even have a say in. I feel like I should have control of my life—and no one else. My parents are my parents, but I'm not some little kid. I'm not eighteen, but I still can think for myself and whether they like it or not, I'm determined. They can work with me or against me; I feel it's their choice.

Oh boy, here comes Barbie and Ken with that other kid, ready to put little Julia in her place.

Who the hell are these people? It looks like they've captured a punked-out Indian. Christ, a green goddamn Mohawk? This is getting weird, like it's a parallel universe or something. I can't believe they've done this to me.

They probably don't know what they've done; somebody must have conned them into it, one of those right wing, stick-up-the-ass friends of theirs. I can't see them coming up with this on their own. Somebody brainwashed them. Probably that Eileen woman Mom hangs out with. I know her: nuts and pushy. But Dad wouldn't listen to her. Of course, if the two of them ganged up on him, nagged him long enough, he might give in. Or maybe they went to a busybody counselor to find out how to control me, then got sold this pile of shit—damn it.

I'm watching the show as they pull out the shears to clip the Mohawk. I wonder if there's a boy or girl under the green bristle. I really can't tell. It doesn't have any chest or much of a butt either. It could be a boy, but it isn't very handsome for a guy. Hey, I don't care. I don't see anybody around here who could hold a candle to Mike. I wish he would hurry up and come get me.

Blue skies, watery eyes, brown dirt.
Things that hurt,
Smiling faces, running races,
Warm sleeping bag
Silent moment
No one to nag.

CHAPTER 8

JULIA

I 've got a tarp, all tied up with a rope and filled with outdoor gear, which they tell me is my "personal responsibility." Like that's supposed to make it important to me somehow. I can't hardly lift it. I get it up by slinging the rope end over my shoulder, stooping down to swing the pack up on my back. I stand up straight using the puny muscles of my skinny legs. If I lean forward a little, I can keep it from rolling off my back when I walk. That's how I carry it, always trying to keep the bundle on my back, stopping when it rolls off to one side or the other. Then I pick it back up off the ground and go through the whole stooping-slinging-hoisting thing every couple hundred feet. It takes almost an hour to get from the road where the van dropped us off to their so-called campsite.

The counselor, Amy, comes with us, but she has a tube framed backpack that she carries like it's nothing. Every time one of us stops to get our pack back on, she stops, watches, doesn't say anything, and doesn't do anything to help us either. I ask why I can't get a backpack like hers, but she gives me some bullshit about me earning one, so I let it go.

When we reach the camp, I'm really tired from carrying all that stuff the half mile from the van. There's three boys and one girl cooking around the fire. Two guys and a woman watch them from a few feet away. I figure they're the jailers.

The first thing I see about the desert camp is it looks bare. I mean there's nothin' there. A bunch of kids sit around a fire with these big tin cups eatin' mush out of them with wood sticks. They don't even have seats or anything. It's not a big fire like it could make you warm or anything. Well, it isn't that cold but still. Then there's a row of tents made out of tarps like the one I wrapped my stuff in. That's it. Outside of that stuff, there isn't anything but some grubby bushes that look half dead in the middle of lots and lots of brown dirt and rocks. Everybody's dressed in the same clothes as me, except they aren't clean like mine. I wear the hiking boots and fresh clothes they gave me: khaki pants and a green short sleeve shirt. The clothes make me scratch and itch all over. I'm pretty sure the boots are already giving me a blister.

That's how I walk into camp with Green Mohawk, who doesn't look so good without the headdress and has the same trouble as me carrying the pack, but it never speaks a word to me or Amy.

I recognize one of the men from Edelman's office. He acts like he's in charge. He comes over to shake hands with Amy. She tells him I'm Julia and Green Mohawk is Katie. The guy is huge, at least six feet tall, a little whiskery with long brown hair, a kid's face, but shoulders like those bulls you see in the rodeos. I guess him to be around twenty-five. He says he's Mark, then he takes Katie and me over to the campfire where he tells everybody who we are, and names all their names. I can't remember any of them.

Amy asks me if I'm hungry. I say I am, so she tells me to get my tin cup out of my pack. It isn't really a tin cup. I mean it's coated with some blue stuff with white speckles like some of the pots my grandma has. I open the pack, get it out. They give me some seeds and grain in it and tell me to cook it over the fire with some water. "Ten grain," they call it. It looks like chicken feed to me. When I ask where the water is, they tell me to get it out of my pack too. Nobody talks to me when I get up to the fire, but they do look me over pretty good.

The cup gets hot real fast when I put it in the fire. When it starts to burn my fingers, I can't hold onto it. I spill half of it. After that I don't get it so close, besides, the smoke seems to follow me no matter where I go around the fire, and it stings my eyes. It takes a while to warm up the mess in the cup, then I ask Amy for a fork or spoon. She tells me to find a good stick to eat it with. I look at the other kids; they have wooden spoons that look like they're carved. I can't find a stick that works so I put a couple sticks together like chopsticks but use them more like a shovel. There isn't much taste. It smells like oatmeal and most of the seeds are still hard, but I eat it all 'cause I'm pretty hungry.

When we finish eating, everybody scoops up some dirt and sand in their cups, mix it up with water, and stir it with their sticks—that's how we wash out the cups. I do what they do and rinse my cup really good, and use up all my water.

"Where can I get more water, Amy?" I ask.

"Back where the van dropped us off. There's three water jugs. You need to go back and get them."

"All the way back there?" I'm tired from the first trip lugging my stuff on my back and my right heal is sore. Now she wants me to go back and get the water.

"Yes, Julia, and get all three of the jugs. We're going to need them before the night is over. Everybody will need more water for the trail tomorrow."

"Why do I have to do it? Why can't somebody else do it? That's a long way to haul those water jugs."

"The others have their assignments. This is yours. Get going."

I look back down the path we came on to see a pile of supplies where the van had been. I can feel the eyes of the other kids watching to see what I'm going to do. I think about refusing to do it, but I don't know what the downside is. Mark is staring at me. I feel outnumbered, so I turn and start walking for the water.

It's a lot easier walking back without the pack on my back, and it's downhill too. The water is in soft plastic jugs about the size of a school backpack, and they're heavy. Each jug has two red plastic handles, like maybe they're for two people to carry. I grab both handles on the first one, but I can barely get it off the ground. I don't know how much it weighs. I weigh ninety pounds. It feels like the jug weighs as much as me. I know it doesn't, but it's heavy. I can't hold it up off the ground so I have to get in front of it, then kinda swing it along by lifting it up a little and sorta throwing it forward. That's how I get it up the hill to the camp. Lift, swing, pull — lift, swing, pull—over and over. By the time I get back with the water, I'm feeling done in.

"Thanks, Julia. You can fill your water bottle from the jug, then go back for the other two," Amy says.

"What for? There's plenty of water here, we don't need those others."

"We need them for tomorrow. Everybody will need water to cook with in the morning and fill up for the hike tomorrow."

"Well, why don't they go get the rest of the water?"

She goes, "They're doing their work, you need to do yours."

I look around. Everybody else is either reading or writing in a notebook. Doesn't look like any of them are doing any work of any kind. I see one of the boys watching us with a smirk on his face. I get the feeling I'm getting the business. The newbie's getting the treatment. I give Amy the meanest look I can without saying anything, turn around, stand up as tall as I can manage, and head back down the hill. I'm pretty much feeling sorry for myself at this point.

I make up my mind to get through this. It takes me an hour to bring the other water jugs to camp. I drag the last one half the way. When it's over, I sit down and turn my back on all of them. I lean back against my pack with my arms around my knees to watch the sun sink down behind some low clouds leaving a warm red and orange glow in the sky. I zone on the sunset. It feels good to watch it, not thinking of anything for a while. Not thinking of where I am. Not thinking of how I hate being here. It's like hypnotic. Nobody bothers me. Then Amy comes over.

"Good job, Julia," she says. I don't trust her encouragement or the smile. "C'mon, I'll help you put up a shelter for the night."

I wonder what she's up to now. Is the initiation over or is this part of it? In spite of myself, I go with it and let it make me feel a little better. While we work, I look her over. She's probably in her twenties—pretty— in a healthy way. She has a lot of hair. I mean really thick, shiny, reddish brown hair that she pulls back in a pony tail. She could make a great model for a health food company, like one of those athletes they always have on the front of a Wheaties box staring at you while you eat your cereal, giving you the look like they just won a goddamn Olympic fucking gold medal. She's being nice though and helpful, and she makes me feel kinda secure. She knows exactly what to do. We unpack the tarp, then she shows me how to tent it. We smooth out a spot on the ground inside for my sleeping bag.

"It'll be dark soon, Julia. It doesn't take long to go from twilight to pitch black out here. It'll be cold too. You should get ready to climb in your bag and go to sleep. I'll be right here in the tent next to you. See you in the morning."

I sit down at the entrance of the tent, untie my bootlaces, pulled off the boots, then the socks and rub my sore feet. I watch the sun wink out behind the top of the hills. No green flash. I don't believe in the green flash, but I always look for it anyway. Some boys told me they saw it, but you can't believe most of what teenage boys tell you. They're usually messin' with your head. Always trying to figure out if you're going to let them get in your pants. That's about all they think about. I never believed they saw the green flash, but I can't help it and look anyway.

It's not really cold, but I shiver and look around at the emptiness. It looks totally bone dead dry at first, but when I focus on some of the details, it doesn't look quite so bare seeing it from ground level. I watch tiny black bodies make a two-way trail between a round ant hill and what looks like a dragonfly corpse. A yellowish lizard is frozen in pose on a small rock pile until I toss a stone at him. It misses, but he slithers under. A hundred feet away, a rabbit nibbles on the one green leaf on a tiny bush sprout.

I slide into the sleeping bag with my clothes on. I roll up a jacket for a pillow so my head isn't falling off my shoulders on the ground. The ground hurts my shoulder and my hip, but I only notice it until my body warms the bag—and I go right to sleep.

Trapped in a box without any key,
The light from a crack is the little I see.
There must be a way for me to break free,
The struggle is different for them and for me.

CHAPTER 9

JULIA

I hate waking up like this with my face in the dirt, knowing I'm stuck out in the middle of no-damn-where, sleeping on rocks, dressed like a gas station attendant, and pooping in a hole. I lift my arms over my head, stretch out my stiff muscles, and whine to myself about losing an all night struggle with the hard-packed ground. I make two fists with my uplifted hands, then shake them at the clear sky—the action changes my mood from sad to mad. A pain spike stops me from turning my head too far right and something throbs at a spot at the top of my hip. I stretch out the waistband of my pants, suck in my belly, and look down there to see a blue-black welt the size of a walnut. It hurts like hell.

The cold morning air flushes goose bumps up my bare arms. I wrap myself in the wool blanket they gave me. I can feel the sun, barely over the horizon, as it warms the icicle tip of my nose. A mild wind blows my dirty, scraggly hair around my head, into my face and forces me to chase it away with one hand while I hold the blanket tight at my throat with the other. I feel dirty.

Mark tells us to line up for our breakfast portion of ten-grain. A small fire warms a pot at his feet. The aroma of coffee mixes with the stinging bite of wood smoke where I take my place with the others. I can't shake the feeling that I've been thrown into the lake with a school of losers.

They move like zombies. I probably look as bad. I would have turned down an offer to look in a mirror, even if one appeared by a miracle in my hand, which doesn't happen anyway. I can't believe I have to put up with these creeps. I'm sure my dad has no idea where he put me, because this scene is the opposite of their usual boring plans for me. Like when they sent me to private school with all those cookie-cutter preppies: "Aren't we the coolest and better than everybody else because our dads are money machines, and we'll never have to worry about anything more important than who has the bigger house or shiniest monstrosity of an SUV." I'm so happy to be done with that crowd, but now this, the other side of the moon. If they caught me hanging out with these guys back home, they'd have a heart attack. My dad would be trying to scare them off with his stupid questions and evil eye. He could run off full-grown adults with that stare. I'd give anything to get a dose of it right now. I'm thinking I might fake my own version to keep these idiots away from me.

I get in line behind Katie of the green Mohawk. Now I'm not an uptight judgmental bitch who puts a whole lot of value on appearances and stuff like that, but...a green Mohawk? I wouldn't've even looked at this kid back home, but here I am living this nightmare. She keeps brushing the palm of her hand over the leftover bristle on the top of her head like she's trying to get it to grow back. Sometimes the kids with the weirdest, most outlandish appearance are quiet and shy when you talk to them. I kinda get that she's not a lesbian, not that I have anything against lesbians, but the way she looks dressed in her boy scout uniform and the shaved head, does give off that vibe. When I look around at the rest of the choices, this girl looks to be the only one who has any chance of becoming a friend if I have to stay here too long.

"How'd it go last night, Katie?" I say to the back of her semi-bald head.

She turns halfway around to look at me over her shoulder, like she isn't sure if I'm talking to her, then brushes the top of her head again. The green dye stripe on the bristle gives her a funny savage look. All she needs is a little face paint on her cheeks and a feather headdress.

She looks me over from head to toe like she's never seen me before. "OK I guess." She has clear blue eyes that contrast with the bright green stripe.

"Well, I couldn't sleep all night with the damn rocks poking me in the shoulder through that stupid sleeping bag," I say. "And my arm is sore from sleeping on it instead of a pillow."

"Oh," she says, before she turns her back on me.

I try again. "Looks like you and I are going through this together since we came out on the same day. These other kids must've been here awhile before us, don't ya think?"

"I didn't do anything bad," she says. "I don't think I'll be here very long." The denial comes at me loud and clear so I give it up. She's at the front of the line anyway.

When it's my turn, I hold out the cup to Amy, who scoops grain out of a sack with the same kind of white speckled blue porcelain cup I have. Who the hell thinks eating chicken feed is going to make us better people? I guess this is somebody's idea of health food or maybe it's their cheap way of keeping us fed so they can make more money off our parents. It's disgusting. Even us vegetarians like some flavor in our food.

"How'd you sleep Julia?"

"Terrible."

She stops shoveling chicken feed to look up at me. She looks all neat and fresh, like she's perfectly comfortable in this godforsaken place. I don't look away when she looks me straight in the eyes.

"You know what, Julia? Attitude is everything out here. You can fight it or work with it. Go against the wind or have it at your back. Whichever you choose, it won't change where you are or what you're doing, but attitude can make this a learning experience or an unbearable misery. Your call. Now what was so terrible about last night?"

I don't need a lecture. "Don't you guys have any pillows?"

"I'll show you how to make one from the stuff in your kit so you won't have a sore neck tomorrow. If you want any more food, ask. It's all the same, but there's plenty of it. You'll want a good supply of energy for the hike today."

I don't answer, give her my best evil eye, take the cup of grain, and turn from her. I sit down on the dirt away from the others and pull the blanket tighter around me.

"Good morning," drips down to me like honey from a jar. I look up at the girl standing next to me. "I didn't get to talk to you yesterday when you got here. I'm Chastity."

Chastity! Oh—my—God. Who the hell names their kid, Chastity? It must be like living your whole life with a piece of toilet paper stuck to the bottom of your shoe. She has a blemish-free face framed in golden blonde hair.

"Julia," I say, then look back down at my cup of mush.

"Mind if I sit down with you?"

"Free country."

"Hey, I know you're going through first day shock, but believe me, it's not all that bad." She sits down next to me, then folds her long legs in front of her Indian-style. "You have to follow their rules, talk to their therapists, and do a lot of hiking—but you'll get used to it."

"I don't want to get used to it. I want out of here."

"There isn't any place to go, so might as well make the best of it."

"What are you doing here?"

"Boy trouble. My parents didn't like Brad."

"They sent you here because they didn't like your boyfriend?"

"They wanted me to break up with him, but he wouldn't let me."

"So you got this?"

"I wasn't trying to break up with him either, so they forced it."

I could see why the guy liked her. Long blonde hair, pretty face, and a perfect figure.

"Assholes!" I say.

She stops eating.

"Well, they aren't all that bad. I kinda understand. What happened was we went to Vegas for the conference play-offs. Cheerleaders on one bus, football team on another. We won the cheerleader competition, but the boys got into some beer the night before the game. They tanked on the field. There was so much confusion about the time we were supposed to leave for home that Brad and I skipped out and got a room. When they counted heads on the bus, the chaperones called the police and made a big deal about finding us. After two days in that hotel room, we turned on the TV. That's when we saw our pictures on the news. Boy, did we freak. This is what I get for turning us in. Brad was expelled and sitting out the rest of the year on probation. My parents tried to get him for statutory rape, but I won't testify. I think that was what made them mad enough to send me here. My dad is really mad. I think I could have gotten around my mom, but he was way pissed."

Her story makes her a lot more likable, somehow less of a stranger. I'm feeling sorry for acting so rude at first.

"So what can I expect for the rest of the day?"

"Well, as soon as we finish breakfast, we break camp and hit the trail. We'll all work together except for Kevin. You'll see."

She finishes her breakfast, then goes off to clean her cup with dirt and water. I follow her lead.

"Everybody get it together," shouts Mark. "We're off to Camp Viper. I want us to get there well before dark."

Everybody has a metal frame backpack but me and Katie. We tie our stuff up in our tarps again, so we can haul it over our shoulders.

"Julia and Katie, get over here."

Mark hands each of us a paper.

"I want you two to memorize these rules. If you can recite them by heart, you'll get a backpack like the rest of us at the next food drop. It can be easily done in a day or so while we hike. Believe me, you're going to want that backpack."

Oh God, here's what I need, more fucking rules. Is there anybody who doesn't have rules for me? I'm sick of it. I stick the paper in my back pocket. The boys are already packing things up. Amy calls me and Katie over to take down the main shelter. It has four corner poles around a center pole holding up a tarp with ropes and stakes. When I take the center stick out, the nylon falls down on my head, blinding me for a second with the pole in my hands. I get a little startled, spin around, and hit Katie in the shoulder with the pole. We're both under the tent, and she comes at me from behind.

"What the hell's the matter with you?" she shouts and hits me open handed on the left side of my face. The slap almost knocks me down. A sharp sting and red heat rise in my cheek.

"Hey, it was an accident," I say. I turn to face her and swing the pole in a swift arc, hitting her about waist high. The recoil on my end tells me I landed a good blow. She jumps me, and we both go down. Katie grabs a handful of my hair. Since she has no hair, I slap her face, trying to make her let go. We roll into one of the corner poles, and the rest of the tarp comes down on us. I hear one of the boys shout, "Girl fight!"

She has my hair, but her other hand gets tangled up in the tarp. I try to loosen the hair grip with my right hand and push her away with the palm of my left on her face. She tries to bite me, but I'm on top of her, so I hold her head on the ground with her face in the dirt.

I know Amy and Mark are trying to find us under the tarp because I feel it being tugged away. Mark yanks me from behind by both arms and lifts me off. Katie gets in one last good kick to my sore hip as Amy pulls her away. She glares at me and shouts "Bitch."

"You're crazy," I say.

"Stay away from me, bitch."

"That's enough," shouts Amy.

"Take her to the trail head." Mark tells Amy. "Julia, this is not the way you are going to act here." He spins me around so we're face to face.

"She started it," I say. "It was an accident. I was only defending myself."

"I don't care who started it. We are not going to solve any problems in this group with physical violence. You got it?"

"If she comes at me again, I will defend myself."

"There'll be no more fighting." He holds me by both shoulders, and we lock eyes for a moment.

"You better keep her away from me," I say as I shake my arms to get loose from his grip. He lets it go and backs away.

"Now help me break this shelter down and stay away from Katie."

We have the attention of all the others. Mark tells them, "Never mind Julia and Katie, do your jobs. We leave in ten minutes."

"Keep *her* away from *me*," I say.

"You aren't going to have the last word, Julia," Mark says. "Do as I say. Grab the corners of this tarp. We'll talk about this later."

I don't care what they think of me, but I hadn't planned on being a problem right off the bat. I mean, I'm hoping to lay low, cruise through this and get out of here in record time. What the hell *is* this? I've never been a fighter. Oh, maybe with my sister, but sisters always do that stuff. Outside of her, I can't remember ever fighting like that with anyone. So they've gotten the wrong impression of me from the start. Shit! Oh well. I'm not going to be who they want me to be if I have to kiss Pocahontas' ass to get there. That little bitch is going to be a problem. I hope they're smart enough to keep her away from me. She isn't my favorite person anyway, and here I am, I've only been here twenty-four hours and I have a damn enemy to deal with. Jeez-us Christ, what's next?

INTERLUDE

STEVEN

Hours later, we were still in my conference room. The angle of the afternoon sun moved to match the slant of the window blinds and a powerful yellow light hit Julia in the face like an interrogator's naked bulb. When she lifted her hand to block it, I got up to close the slats.

"So that's how I felt when I first got there. Mad and abandoned. What else do you want to talk about, Dad?" Julia asked, as I sat back down on the other side of the table facing her.

It seemed to be getting easier for her to open up about everything. I fiddled around with the recorder for a minute to make sure it was still recording.

"Let's talk about the letters; we wrote a lot of them; we probably have the record for the most letters between a father and daughter ever," I said. I spoke with some authority on this because I had kept all of hers. Mine were drafted on a word processor, so I had a file containing those too. There were at least a hundred of them, counting mine and hers.

"You know the letters I wrote you were mostly bullshit, right?" she said, as she pulled the pins out of her bun and let her hair fall in waves over her shoulders.

"What do you mean by that?"

"I self-censored, Dad. If I wrote anything in there about what it was really like, they would make me re-write it. After going through a couple of forced re-writes, I only wrote about day-to-day stuff and nothing about how I really felt. It was awful, Dad. You have no idea what you put me into. That's what I was thinking; you and Mom had no idea about what I was going through, and I couldn't tell you because they wouldn't let me. I felt scared and alone."

"I'm sorry, Julia. You know I didn't want to hurt you. I wanted to save you."

My secretary opened the door and looked in.

"Hi, Julia. Sorry to interrupt, Steven. You have several callers waiting to hear back from you. Is there anything I can do?"

I checked my watch. "Please tell everyone I'm in a meeting for the rest of the day and cancel my four o'clock with Mercer. See if he can reschedule for Monday. I'll return all the calls in the morning."

She nods, gives Julia a smile, and closes the door behind her.

"Don't get me wrong about the letters. They were very important to me. I needed them. I think I got more letters from you guys than the other kids got from their parents."

"That was my goal," I said. "I knew the letters would let you know you were loved."

"There was one kid there who never got any letters. Sometimes I let him read mine."

"I remember a couple of letters where you wrote about a kid that wanted to eat a bird," I said. "Was that the kid?"

"No, that was Sam. I'll tell you about Sam."

My Candy Coated Life
Strip off the sugar coating,
Pull off the frosting shingles,
Peel away the ginger bread walls,
Wipe up the whip cream floors.
All that's left standing
Are the windows and the doors.
No where to go
No where to hide
Let yourself out and others inside.

CHAPTER 10

JULIA

I walk head down, bending forward to counterbalance the weight of my pack. We hike in a cloud, dust kicked up from the hard pan of baked dirt by the heels of our boots.

When I pick my head up, all I see is brittle manzanita leaves that curl in the dry heat. Snakes and green lizards move in slow motion under wilted bushes searching for bugs or any tiny drop of water. Grass doesn't grow here. The scrub oaks are thin, their dark green leaves singed brown at the edges by the burning sun. Fat trunks and stubby limbs that gave up trying to grow tall or long, life knocked down by daytime heat, bitter cold nights, and withering desert dust storms. We're hoping the dark clouds on the horizon mean there's a storm coming.

The counselors have prepared us for rain. My gear is wrapped in a brown tarp with my red one-gallon water bottle tied on top. I have a blue tarp over my clothes, tied snug around my waist with a rope sash. The first rain comes all of a sudden in a thick downpour. I'm glad to have the cover, but the sudden humidity makes me sweat under my rain clothes when the sun peeks out between showers. Most of the time, I look down at my boots as I walk. There's nothing else to see really, except for Sam trudging along in front of me. I watch him pick up rocks and throw them at trees and bushes as we go along. Sometimes a lizard slithers away as we approach, and Sam tries for it. The air is silent.

Sam is the skinniest boy I've ever seen. I mean, I'm skinny, but this kid could slip through the spaces in a picket fence. He's kind of a hippie. You know: back to nature, live off the land, all that stuff. Kinda goofy too. I kinda like him. I mean, not like I *like* like him, you know, more like an easy friend. He strikes me as pretty harmless and sorta gentle. That's what I like about him. We aren't supposed to talk while we hike, but I have a quiet talk going on with Sam as we trudge along. I'm surprised when he tells me he's going to kill a bird.

"See the bird on that pine tree up ahead?" Sam says over his shoulder. "When we get there, I'm gonna knock him down with this rock."

"Why do you want to hurt the poor bird, Sam? Leave him alone."

"I'm gonna eat him. I'm gonna hit him in the head with this rock, knock him down, and eat him. It's the law of the jungle. I haven't had any meat for days. I'm so tired of ten grain."

"Yeah right. First of all, you'll never hit him; second, even if you did, there's not enough meat on that bird to make a mouthful."

It's a woodpecker: clean white breast, black speckled wings, with a red cap on the back of his head like one of those dome caps you see some Jewish guys wear to cover their bald spots. I watch him pecking at the bark half way up a sorry looking pine tree. He moves sideways around the trunk. You can't see his head move, but you can hear the sharp taps in short strings of fast picks. "Di-di-di-dit. Di-di-di-dit." He's a pretty guy. I don't want Sam to hurt him, but I really don't think there's a chance in hell he can hit him. Sam picks up rocks and sorts through them as we get closer. When he finds one he likes, he tosses it up and down in front of him as he walks.

"This one will do it. I can feel it," he says. His eyes are focused on the bird. He slows a little as we approach and holds his arm straight out behind him to signal me to stay back.

"Don't do it, Sam," I say.

"Shhh…you'll scare him away. Shut up," he whispers over his shoulder.

The bird is far enough off the trail that it doesn't spook when the line of hikers goes by. Everyone sees him. They all turn to the sound—"Di-di-di-dit"—and you can't miss the red dot and bright white patch in the middle of all the browns and dull greens. When Sam reaches the closest point, he stops to cock his arm for the throw. He throws so hard he loses his balance under the weight of his pack and stumbles forward a few steps, but he doesn't go down. I watch the rock spinning in a low arc and hold my breath. It catches the pecker right behind his red cap with a crack. He falls motionless to the ground. Sam freezes for a minute, looks at me with a wide-eyed grin, jumps and strikes the air with his fist, then lets out a shrill whoop, patting his mouth with the palm of his hand, the warble of the Indian war cry. He runs to the tree where he picks up the black and white body and holds it high in one hand like an athlete's prize. Then he stomps round and round in a clumsy victory dance and shouts, "Bull's eye, dinner, dinner, dinner, I got dinner."

The rest of the troop stops and surrounds Sam. Mark steps in immediately, grabs the arm that holds the trophy, and pries the bird out of his hand.

"Hey, what are you doing with my bird? I hunted it and killed it and it's mine."

"We're not going to hunt or kill anything. Why did you do this?" Mark asks him.

"I want some meat, that's why. All you guys give us is ten grain. I want some meat, and I'm going to eat this bird. I killed it, and it's mine. Give it back." Sam reaches for the bird, but Mark holds it behind his back.

"No, Sam, nobody's going to eat this bird. Who knows what diseases it carries? We aren't out here to hunt or kill animals, and we're only going to eat things we know are safe. There's no doctor within miles. We can't risk you getting sick."

"Aw, c'mon. Can't you let us have a little fun? Do you have to control everything? You guys are a bunch of uptight assholes."

"Shut it, Sam. Everybody back on the trail. We have two more hours to go to get to camp tonight. I don't want to do it in the dark. Get going. Now!"

Mark takes the bird off the trail, scrapes a shallow grave with the heal of his boot, and buries it. Sam watches him, deflated after the thrill of the kill.

"Let's go, Sam," I say. "You know you can't fight them and win."

"I wanted a little meat, that's all."

"It isn't fair, but then what's fair out here anyway?" I say.

We get in line on the trail behind the others. I feel different about Sam now. I mean I don't think the bird thing is all that bad really. I feel sorry for the bird, but after seeing Sam so excited, then defeated by Mark, I feel a little closer to him, like I know something real about him. Sam acts different too. He's the kid who kills birds with a stone for Chrissake. He has cred. The tribe gives him more respect. I kinda think Katie is a little attracted to him even though she tries not to show it. The boys stop teasing him and treating him like a geek. I don't tease him anymore either.

Mark is on the trail ahead of me when I see him pick up something from the side of the track. He turns and hands me a black rock. "Take this, you'll need it. Be careful of the edge, it's sharp."

It's shiny and smooth with a knife-edge, like a chunk of black glass.

"It's obsidian, volcanic glass from a lava flow. You'll find it all over around here. When these mountains were active volcanoes, they spit this stuff out as a hot liquid that cooled into pieces of glass. It breaks like glass, and the broken shards are harder than man-made glass, sharper than a surgeon's scalpel. The Coquille Indians used it to make tools and weapons. You can carve a spoon with it. It'll be better than eating with a stick."

Mark looks around him on the ground until he finds a scrap of tree branch.

"Here's a piece of madrone. See how it's wide at this end? Carve that out, and you can make the scoop part of the spoon. Whittle the other end down to make a handle however you want it."

"I'm supposed to make a spoon out of this?" I say.

"Well, it's up to you. You can keep eating with a stick, or you can make a spoon. It's not as hard as it looks. You have to work it slowly and give it some time." He shows me how to use the edge of the stone to scrape the wood away and how to cut with the sharp edge in a chipping motion. Then he hands me the two pieces.

"You can do it," he says.

For some reason, Mark is acting a little nicer today. The first time I saw him and he saw me, he hardly spoke to me. When he did finally say something the second day, he was so mean.

"Get over here with your pack, Julia. I'll show you how to pack it properly," he said.

He made me unpack everything out of the stupid tarp, even my underwear; I was so embarrassed. Then I had to put it all back the way he told me.

"Not like that, pack it tight. If the stuff in your pack moves around while you walk, it'll make your hike harder. You don't want to spend your energy shifting this stuff back and forth. Are you listening to me?"

I didn't say anything. He kinda scared me. I put it all back the way he said, then he showed me how to tie it up with loops in the rope for my arms. When I hiked that day, it was easier like he told me it would be. He didn't have to treat me like that.

Eating with my fingers and a stick isn't fun. I decide to try making a spoon. I'm thinking that having a spoon, even a rough wooden imitation would be better. We turn back to the trail, and I follow Mark. I try working the wood with the stone while I walk, but it's too hard to hold it steady and scrape it. When I cut my finger, I decide to wait for a rest stop.

I'm a far cry from where I was a week ago. I never imagined I'd be missing having a spoon. Guess there are a lot of things I took for granted before, but I know this is a temporary setback, and I'm going to make it through my way.

It isn't what you'd call whittling, but the stone is hard and sharp enough to scrape and shape the piece of wood he gave me. After a few rest stops, I have a pretty good spoon carved out. It makes me anxious for dinner. The hike makes me way starving and dead tired.

***

My eyes sense light through my closed lids. I can tell the blue sky has started to glow and can't decide if I should open my eyes and face reality— or keep them closed and try to escape back into my sleep world. I decide the dreams are worse. Without moving my head, I let my blurry eyes open and scan the horizon. A soft glow comes into focus at the edge of the desert, then the wink and flash of a fuzzy yellow disk breaking the horizon triggers me. I sit up in my sleeping bag and rummage through my belongings for a piece of string to tie my hair. Everything is dirty: my face, my hair, my hands, my gear. Tying the string around my wind-knotted hair feels good and somehow cleansing.

I rub my eyes. The dream was awful. I'd run away and couldn't find my way home. Some people started following me—then more and more people—like I was at the head of an angry mob. They started yelling and screaming. I started to run, and they ran after me. When I looked back, they were all my teachers, our neighbors, and a squad of policeman. They were all angry, shaking their fists and shouting. Mike found me and whisked me away. I told him I wanted to go home, and he said, "Forget about that, this is your home." He tried to have sex with me, but I wouldn't let him, and I heard my dad talking to my mom about me in the next room as if I was dead. I finally got home, but there was no one there except my sister, and she told me my parents had died of a broken heart.

I take a deep breath, shake my head and focus on the reality about me to get the dream out of my mind.

We're spending the day in camp. The white van brings us supplies, and there's mail. Mark hands me three letters from my dad. They were sent a week before, mailed two days apart by the postmarks. I don't open them. I'm kinda glad to get them, but they make me think about how they've been so mean to leave me here. I really don't want another lecture, and I especially don't want to read about how I 'm on the wrong path and all that shit. Seeing these letters makes me feel like crying but I don't. I put them in one of my pants' pockets.

He never had anything good to tell me when I was home, so why should I want to hear from him now—after he leaves me here? Like I'm so bad they can't deal with it? I never did anything to them, except tell them off maybe. Well, that's words. It didn't hurt anyone. Oh, I know what's in those letters, more bullshit about how my friends aren't real friends, they're leading me astray, and I'm some kind of gullible moron following along. That's crap. I make my own choices, and nobody tricks me into doing anything.

Kevin comes over to me and asks what's in my letters. It's the first time we've had more than a couple of words. He usually stays all to himself and doesn't say anything, like he's deep in thought all the time. He stands there with his hands in his pockets, shifting his chubby body back and forth from one foot to the other. His round face looks at me through soft brown puppy eyes, and I can't lose the impression that his wild, uncombed red hair makes it look like his head is on fire.

"I don't know. I didn't read them."

"Why not?" he says, "Don't you want to hear from your parents? Mine never write to me. They're probably too busy. You know, with business and stuff. You should read your letters."

"What do you care? How old are you?"

"I'm thirteen. I've been here for five months. It's OK. I don't care if I stay here or not. If you're not going to read your letters, can I read one?"

"No, they're personal."

"How do you know? You didn't even open them."

"Now you're getting annoying. Why have you been here so long? I'm going to get out of here as fast as I can."

"Here, home—what's the difference? Why should I play their stupid game so I can go back home where it's as boring as here?"

"But anything is better than here."

"Well you've never lived at my house."

"You don't make sense."

"That's what everybody says about me. Everybody hates me because I don't want to do anything, and don't care about their stupid program, and don't care if I ever get out of here."

"I don't hate you. I said you're annoying, that's all. Look, maybe I'll read the letters later; then maybe I'll let you read one, I'll see."

"OK," he says and walks off with the kind of waddle that short people with big bums have. It makes me smile, and I think I might share one of the letters with him later.

We unload the supplies, then they tell us to work at making a fire. It isn't exactly rubbing two sticks together, but it's close. You'd think the brush around here would light up by spontaneous combustions, everything being so hot and dry. But no, we have to make a fire. Another piece of nonsense I have to put up with to get them to let me go home. I ask Sam to help me, but I find out right away he doesn't have a clue. It's this Jimmy D. guy that shows me.

Jimmy D. is like most boys my age, pretending to be something he's not. I think boys get all that macho stuff from movies. Girls know it's make believe, but boys—they're too stupid to realize it. He sees himself as a gangster, but his slick front is easy to see through. Still, it makes me wary. The one thing about him I know isn't phony is he can rap. Not imitation rap, real original stuff. He may be the only white guy I will ever meet who wishes he was born black. I'm not kiddin'. He told me. He says he has the rhythm, and he has the beat, and he should have been born black.

"You don't have to be black to be a rapper. There's white rappers."

"Yeah, but those guys have money and producer connections behind them. They're manufactured celebrities; they don't have the soul in them."

"You're makin' excuses."

"OK bitch, listen to this."

Jimmy stands up and backs away from me. He's almost six feet tall, lanky with a buzz cut that's grown out to a spiky looking blonde fur. His face gets all serious, and he poses with that unnatural rapper stance with odd angled arms and open finger gestures.

> Why you think you here?
> Did you daddy make it clear?
> He don't want you messin' round
> W'da beastie boys in town.

You done broke d'gol'en rule.
An you skippin' outa school,
So now you gotta pay,
Til' you walk the righteous way.
So don' try 'n put me down,
Like some ordinary clown,
I can talk a freakin' story
That'll make you feelin' sorry.
Get the doubtin' out yo' head
And the truth in what I said
 Remember where you are
When I'm rappin' like a star..."

I wave my hands in front of Jimmy to make him stop and get back to working with me on the fire thing. I have to admit I'm impressed, but my admiration is short lived when he starts bragging about his exploits.

"I got lotsa black friends, and we're brothers. We do stuff together—on the street."

"Like what?"

"Well, we stole a car."

Sam listens to us as he works alone on his own fire kit. He giggles when he hears this.

"What's funny Sam?" I ask.

"Jimmy fuckin' D took his mom's Cadillac for a joy ride with his underage cousin and drove across the state line before they got caught. He'd be going to jail as a sex offender if his momma hadn't begged the judge to sending him here instead."

"That's it? You took your mom's car and diddled your cousin?"

"Look, we can do stuff."

"OK, Jimmy, you're a tough guy. OK, so do you know how to make a fire? I need to know how to do it so I can get outa here," I say.

"Go kill a canary Sam. This is none a your business." Jimmy turns back to me. "You got your rig?"

"No, I don't—*got my rig.*" I say. Then I'm sorry I mocked him because I need his help, but he lets it go.

He pulls out a bundle wrapped in a piece of tarp from his backpack and hands it to me. I open it to find a straight stick, a curved piece strung with cord like a tiny bow for shooting tiny arrows and a flat piece.

"This is what you're gonna need to bow drill a fire. Do you have a piece of obsidian to work it?"

I show him the piece Mark gave me.

"That'll do. Now find a piece of softwood for the spindle. Get the straightest piece of sage you can find and scrape it smooth like mine." He shows me a piece of wood that has the shape of a long skinny cigar. It's smooth and straight, obviously polished, rounded at one end and a blunt point at the other.

We rummage around the area. I find a straight piece I think will work. Jimmy gets Mark to let him use a hicksaw, a dull-bladed, short machete-like tool. He uses it to rough out a curved piece he says will make a good bow and a flat piece of juniper he says will be the hardwood base. Jimmy works with the intensity of someone who knows how to do something well and wants to show off. I take advantage. I work on the spindle with my obsidian tool while he makes the other pieces. When he finishes his parts, and I'm still working, he takes over from me and quickly finishes the spindle.

He makes a little indent in the flat base like a thumb print next to the edge of the board and takes my obsidian tool from me to cut a notch from the dimple to the edge. He sharpens the end of the spindle like a pencil to go into the indent on the base. We have everything ready except for what Jimmy calls "the palm piece." This piece of wood has a dent that fits the rounded upper end of the spindle.

The bow string makes the contraption complete. He ties a piece of camp cord across the bow and twists the string around the spindle. We work together for hours on this. I worry he might give up on me, but he follows through all the way. I think he wants the pay-off as much as me. We both want that fire.

He shows me how to set everything up with the palm piece on top of the spindle, the bow string wrapped on it, and the pointed end of the spindle in the hardwood base. He prepares some dry wood shavings in a pile that looks like a little birds nest. He shows me how to run the bow back-and-forth to make the spindle turn. I work the bow a long time before I can see a red glow at the bottom of the spindle.

"Look, Jimmy, I got a fire."

"That's not a fire yet, keep spinning. I'm gonna try to get that red-hot coal into the kindling shavings."

My hands and arms are getting tired and I want to rest, but I keep the spindle going for fear of losing the coal. Whenever I begin to slow down,

Jimmy yells at me to keep it up. He pokes a stick at the glowing coal until it falls out of the notch at the edge of the board and into his shaving pile. When the coal drops in, he blows on it, and the shaving nest flames up. He moves quickly and starts to rap.

> When the fire's gettin'hot,
> Gotta be there on the spot,
> Don't you let the coal be coolin'
> Or you're a fire foolin'
> A easy little blowin'
> Will get the fire glowin'
> Now we have success
> Ahead of all the res'.

Jimmy drops the burning embers into a larger kindling pile and the fire grows.

"Get me some sticks, and we'll have a nice campfire," he says.

I run to pick up any piece of wood I can find around the camp and throw them on. The fire grows some more. Sam sees our fire and pitches in. The three of us slap our hands in a clumsy high five. Jimmy shows me a contagious smile and yells at Mark. "Hey Mark, come see this. Julia's got her first fire."

CHAPTER 11

STEVEN

A depressive melancholy gripped my spirit the second I crossed the threshold into Julia's room. I scanned the jumble of empty clothes, small and bright, abandoned, fragile, lifeless—cruel confirmations of her forced absence. If she were there, she'd have been fiercely defending her space with every bit of spirit and will. Instead I stood there like a survivor at an estate sale, faced with all the personal pieces of her life. It was a scene she had expected to return to in a few hours. My presence had the feel of a desecration, like stepping on a grave or peeping in a window.

The room had been her oasis, her hide-out, her sanctuary. It was a lively place at times where she took her friends to talk and scheme and play music. It should have been a quiet place to study too, but not much of that went on in there. It felt too quiet, morose. We'd looked in the door over the past few months, but we allowed her the privacy of her own room. With her gone, I felt a guilty shame at taking undefended ground. We were free to explore it, no one could stop us. We performed our duty, but it felt wrong.

Small patches of carpet peeked out here and there from under the layers of cotton and denim. I cleared a narrow path. The feel of the tiny, weightless clothes in my hands triggered a picture of the wearer in my mind.

Her small frame gave her a delicate appearance that masked a resilient strength. She had brown eyes and a pretty face that could light up a room with a smile or bring on a black-out gloom with her frown. Women eyed her with jealousy because of a genetic advantage that kept her effortlessly slim. There was a brown birthmark about the size of a quarter right below her left knee. The stain presented her only visible flaw if you want to think of it that way. I thought of it as giving her character and a thousand times better than any tattoo.

The bed was unmade as expected, and the closet doors stood open exposing more clothes and a pool of mismatched shoes in the bottom. A stereo system hung over the edge of the dresser top, fighting for space with an accumulation of scent bottles and a teetering stack of CDs.

Graffiti covered the walls with a mixture of fun and nasty. Felt pen, crayon, and silver spray paint marked the wall spaces and doors. There were simple signatures, cute sayings, and the little cartoons girls do for each other. The more aggressive stuff made me uncomfortable, but the one that hit me hardest was "Julia is a whore."

I knew who wrote that one. It was Darla. I blamed Darla for a lot of the trouble. She's a controlling person, and she stuck like glue to whomever she got under her spell. Julia was definitely caught. Once Darla had a victim, she knew exactly how to manipulate them. She trapped them in subtle and not so subtle ways, which made them helpless none the less. Once caught, it was as if she had them in a psychic straight jacket.

Darla was the first of Julia's friends to engage in sex, and it gave her a special status.

I know how it works. I remember when I was a teen and heard the gossip about a guy who was having sex with his girl friend. All of a sudden he was out of my class. Somebody who knew what I wanted to learn. Darla enjoyed that exalted position within her sphere. She was constantly touting it and egging on others to be participants like her.

Once I found Darla and Julia and two boys in our hot tub where Darla had pulled Julia's top down. I surprised them and broke up the party. Afterward, I took Darla aside.

"Darla, I don't ever want you in my house or on my property again," I said.

"But it was an accident. We weren't doing anything; please, you're making a mistake." she said with an air of sincerity I knew was false.

"I'm not fooled Darla. I mean it, I don't want you here."

"Well you are just as mean as Julia says you are. I don't care to be here anyway," and she walked away.

I knew I couldn't enforce a demand that she never see Julia, but I could enforce this. Darla never stepped foot in my house again. The few times I did see her outside of our home, she avoided me, and I let her, but she kept her control over Julia.

If Julia tried to get away from Darla, she was barraged by constant phone calls from Darla and mutual friends calling to admonish Julia about being unfair to Darla. I could hear Julia's side of phone conversations through the thin walls between our bedrooms late into the night. The crying and arguing was heart-rending. Darla, of course, told lies about Julia to their friends, Darla's other acolytes, to get them to call.

Eventually, Julia would make up with Darla and beg her forgiveness so she could have peace. Julia seemed to be forced into a repeating cycle of the four temperaments. In the melancholic phase, the critical judgements of her peers drove her into a lonely depression. This was followed by a passive introspection that invariably led to her finding that she was wrong, and Darla was right. With the fighting died down, her compliance allowed relationships to heal and progress to the sanguine, and everything was right with the world again. Each time Julia experienced this cycle, Darla's grip grew stronger. Then Julia feared crossing her even more the next time. I watched it happen. I tried to explain it to Julia, but Darla had caught her. No amount of logical discussion got through to her. It began with an awe of Darla and developed into a fear of Darla; a shark who knew how to deal from the bottom of the deck and run a good bluff.

I imagined Darla with the can of silver spray paint, gleefully writing trashy sayings on Julia's walls while Julia watched helplessly for fear of offending Darla—and becoming the pariah of her social group again. So now we had relegated Julia to the care of strangers because of Darla and some nineteen-year-old sexual predators. I wished I could make them pay for what they'd done to my family. The thought gnawed at my consciousness.

Mary came into the room with a mission. Determined and empowered, she had no reservations like me. She drove for her goal to find Julia's diary. She rummaged through drawers, got on her knees, and searched under the bed. When she did find it, she made herself comfortable sitting against stacked pillows on Julia's bed and settled in for a thorough read-through looking for clues.

She told me intimate details she found out about Julia's experiences with sex and drugs. She offered me the diary to read, but I couldn't bring myself to look at it. Part of me thought it too personal, a violation of Julia's privacy. On the other hand, I had a duty to find out what was going on in her head, and what was going on in her life outside of our family. I made a compromise. I let Mary do the reading, then tell me what she found. Julia's mother reading the diary didn't strike me as quite so bad as having me, her father, reading it.

The diary revealed that our 14-year-old daughter experienced sex with three guys. The facts surprised me. I wasn't shocked. I wasn't "disappointed in her." I was pissed at the nineteen-year-old guys who were taking advantage of her. The diary gave me all the proof I needed to prosecute these guys. They had committed the crime of statutory rape, but without Julia's testimony it wouldn't go far in a court of law. I knew Julia well enough to be certain she'd never testify against them. She would never admit they took advantage of her. She'd already said in her letters that my opinion that these people had manipulated her was wrong. Over and over again, I heard she was completely in control of the situation, she knew exactly what she was doing. She knew the upside and downside, the right and the wrong of it, but she chose to do it anyway. No one influenced her to do these things.

The diary was an eye opener.

A constant search
For who I am
What can I be
Where do I stand?

CHAPTER 12

Julia jumped down from the second-to-last step of the school bus, one of several in a long yellow line that bordered the South High campus. She carried a book-heavy backpack, stopped to swing it onto her shoulders, and settled the straps. Then she joined the stream of students that trickled out of buses and drifted toward the school in their morning trance. Bewildered freshmen tried to remember where their first class met, sophomores looked for a glimpse of their love interest, juniors tried to pull up the theorem or Spanish vocabulary they thought they had mastered the night before, and seniors suffered the start of another boring day on their way to graduation.

Julia looked around at the chaos. The teenage horde rolled over the trim lawn and crisscrossed walkways in the direction of nine-foot-tall double doors at either end of the façade of the neo-gothic school building. The novelty of the first two weeks of school had already worn off, but she still reveled in the freedom the high school environment gave her in contrast to last year's tightly structured middle school. The semi-free environment injected her psyche with an adrenal charge. She spotted Darla right away, with a group of boys under the tall oak at the south end of the lawn.

Darla drew boys like Adam to the apple. She wore a short skirt, heels, and a tight, low-cut top that gave a peek at the swell of her creamy breasts. Heavy make-up tried its best to soften a coarse face, with heavy eyebrows and a thick-lipped, wide mouth over a recessive chin. She compensated for this flaw by showing off the rest of her early maturing body, and she had mastered a come-hither smile that delivered an unmistakable sensual message. Her brown eyes invited easy intimacy.

"Hi, Julia, you are looking especially pretty today," Darla said as Julia approached. The ring of boys opened up to allow Julia in, and she let herself enjoy the compliment in front of the boys.

"Hey, Darla, who're yer friends?"

"This is Mike," Darla said, pointing at a tall dark-haired, lanky boy with a broad smile, "and this is Evan and Carl. They're not in school anymore. They have a house down on Plum Street. They want to know if we'll meet them over there at lunch time."

"Well, I guess so," Julia said. "But I have to run now, or I'll be late for my first class."

"Oh, don't get your panties in a twist over that," Mike said. "School is a pile of crap anyway. They only want you in there so they can get money from the government to pay their salaries. The more kids they can get in their classes, the more money they make. It's all about the headcount."

"Well I'm going in, maybe I'll see you later," Julia said heading for the steps.

"Don't let the bastards grind you down," Mike shouted at Julia as she walked away.

"I'll see you right here at the lunch break," Darla called and turned back to her conversation with the boys.

***

Three hours later, Julia walked down the steps to the school lawn. She saw Darla in the same spot with Mike and Evan. Darla waved at Julia and beckoned her over.

"We waited for you. Let's go, their house is down the street a couple of blocks." Darla said. She looked around, then spoke to Julia, "These guys have some weed to share with us."

"OK, but I only have forty-five minutes before my next class."

"You're taking life too seriously," Mike said. "Come on, let's have some fun."

The group swept Julia along down the street to a bungalow.

"This place looks like a dump," Julia whispered to Darla as they walked up to the front door. "I'm not sure I want to go in there with these guys."

"It's OK Julia, I know these guys. I've been here before. Come-on, relax, it will be fun."

Mike invited them into the small living room. Discarded clothes, unfinished meals on dirty plates, and beverage cans and bottles cluttered the room. The center piece was a powerful stereo system flanked by tall speakers that made a loud pop when Mike hit the amplifier ON switch. High volume notes of a popular love song filled the house. The boys swept the clutter off the couch and made room for the girls to sit. Julia dropped her heavy back-pack on the floor at her feet and settled into the couch next to Darla.

"You guys wanna smoke a bowl?" Mike asked.

"I'm not sure if..." Julia said.

"Well I am," Darla said. "You got any decent weed? The last time I smoked with you guys it was wonder weed—I kept wondering if I was ever gonna get high."

"You are so demanding Darla," Evan said. "This is good stuff, Michoacán. I promise you, you're going to see Jesus."

"I don't think I want to smoke right now," Julia said.

"Oh come on," Mike said. "He's only kidding about seeing God. It's mellow, you'll like it."

The girls watched as Evan went to work with a hair pin, cleaning out a glass pipe. Mike shook some pot out of a baggie onto a magazine cover and removed the stems. Evan handed him the pipe, and he loaded the pot and tamped down the bowl with his finger tip. He lit it with a butane lighter and handed it to Evan. The pipe went from Darla to Julia, who took a tentative draw and coughed out a cloud of white smoke.

"Here, take a sip of this," Mike said and handed her a cold can of beer.

She took the beer and sipped it. The coughing stopped, and she tried to hand it back to him.

"Keep it," he said. "I'll get another one. Do you want one Darla?"

"Is that all we get? I want some of Evan's tequila."

"Whatever Darla wants, Darla gets," Evan said, then disappeared into the kitchen and returned with a square bottle and four shot glasses. "If Darla's gonna do it, we're all gonna do it."

They emptied the half-full bottle in an hour. When Julia decided it was time to go, she stood up too quickly, tripped on her backpack and her legs buckled. Mike caught her and put her back on the sofa. He tossed the backpack in a corner.

"You OK?" he said.

"Just give me a minute, and I'm going to go back to my class."

"Julia, you can't go back to school in this condition. You might as well stay and enjoy it. Let's smoke again. It will take the edge off the tequila," Mike said.

"But I can't miss my class..." Julia said.

"Julia, lighten up, it's just one class. Really!" Darla said.

The pipe went around the room again.

Evan and Darla cuddled at one end of the sofa. Julia watched as Evan slipped his hand between Darla's thighs and up under her skirt. Darla closed her eyes and relaxed into the couch. Evan began kissing her. She didn't resist.

"Let's give them some privacy," Mike said to Julia, took her hand and led her down the hall and into a bedroom. "You are so beautiful," he said. He kissed her and nudged her to sit on the bed.

"I'm a little high," she said.

"That makes it best," Mike said and pushed her back on the bed. He kissed her and slipped his hand up under her blouse.

CHAPTER 13

STEVEN

The diary revelations left me with unwelcome conjectures about my daughter's runaway experience. I hated the imagined pictures that haunted me, like chilling scenes from a violent movie. I guess I went a little crazy with the desire to make someone pay. That's what got me on the road to Jack's place, out in the valley west of town.

I drove out the two-lane highway that runs along the bottom of the Applegate valley. Small caliper evergreen timber spotted the hills on both sides of the road, where the forest tried to recover a semblance of dignity—re-seeding the hills to hide a nakedness clear-cutters exposed before conservation laws came in.

I slowed the car to look out over the forest at the top of Jacksonville hill and thought about finding a spot to turn around. My conscience annoyed me, but I kept on. There are some actions you know for certain you could never take, but there are others you don't know you could do until you do them. I struggled to reconcile my values with my current planned course of action. What would Mary think?

I turned off the noisy radio. The diary had stimulated thoughts of revenge that spoiled my concentration and disturbed me like the squeaky wheel no amount of oil will silence. I've never been the type to let go with an uncontrolled temper. I'm a Libra: mellow, easy, compassionate, but that day I felt like a Taurus, ready to bully with no regrets about it. I toyed with the Yin and the Yang, hesitant about the morality of my plan, knowing I shouldn't do what I was scheming, but emotion possessed me and drove me to act.

I tried to avoid the troublesome rebuttal my conscience gave me by focusing on the beauty of my route. A pass through this valley in the springtime on a sunny day gives one the feeling of driving the length of a miles-long postcard. Every bend presents a new scene: round-top barns, rail fences, tractors sprouting rooster tail dust blows, grazing farm animals, and barking ranch dogs. The fields color themselves in wildflowers; acres of purple vetch, yellow mustard, and orange poppies that dress-up the pastures and hay fields—a cheerful announcement of their annual resurrection.

A tight curve slowed me down, which proved fortuitous for a mother deer and three fawns crossing the road a hundred feet from where I straightened out. I slammed on the brakes. Screeching tires brought me to a full stop as four clueless deer ambled across the road in front of my car, unconcerned about the galloping beat of my heart. An omen? Again I thought to turn around, but only for an instant, and I proceeded on.

The valley exists in a unique reality, out of sync with normal time and space. Miners and farmers, winemakers and cowboys, retirees and trust babies inhabit the hills—the oddest assembly of independent people you will find anywhere. Appearances mean nothing here. The most ragged looking character turns out to be a millionaire, the one arm woman will destroy your ego in a game of eight-ball, and the impeccably dressed guy wearing a silk top hat is a penniless gold miner. I don't remember when we first met Jack, but I think it must have been at the Boom Town Saloon where Mary made friends with local musicians who played jazzed-up rock at the weekend jam session.

Jack fits the stereotype of those native Oregonian woodsmen who view life with a black and white certainty of right and wrong that sometimes triggers actions that no one can foresee or control. I counted on this when I headed out to the woods to find him, and I intended to make something happen that months ago I would have discouraged and condemned if it were the action of any other man. I felt unconstrained by philosophical morality—or the rule of law. I had committed myself to vigilante action, and I meant for the guilty to be punished.

The main highway swerves and dips through the valley, but at the turn-off into the canyon where Jack lives, the experience changes. I bumped over the first washboard cattle guard, crept through a herd of twenty Angus, then over the second guard and onto a track that looked more like a wagon trail than a road. Decomposed granite surfaced the rough path in a few spots, but two parallel dirt grooves with grass growing between them were the main feature that showed the way. The road wound right and left. My car passed madrones with inches to spare and skirted the edge of gullies that forced my trajectory. My path ran under the canopy of a deep wood. Occasional trails went off to the right or left and sometimes a major 'Y' challenged the unfamiliar traveler with a Frostian decision. I'd been out to Jack's place a few times, so with some good guesses and a little luck, I was able to find it without a guide.

When I turned on to Jack's driveway, the road pitched up so steep before the summit, only sky was visible through my windshield, then the hood dipped, and I looked down on Jack's metal-clad mobile home. A barking black Labrador greeted me as I descended into a hollow. I didn't know the dog, but the cyclic wave of his metronome tail assured me he was not a threat. He seemed grateful for my appearance, a break in the quiet monotony of the woods. I got out of the car, and we walked together up to the door of the trailer while he sniffed my boots, and I hollered for his owner.

Jack looked out of the trailer door in response to the Lab's bark and my call. A faded plaid flannel shirt hung loose over his well-worn blue jeans, an appearance that camouflaged a sharp intellect and humorous wit. A broad smile on his unshaven face displayed a gap where his four front teeth should have been. From what I knew of Jack's history, he could have lost the teeth by a prior meth habit, a bar room brawl, or a domestic disagreement with any one of several of the fiery girl friends he'd jilted along the way.

Despite the fact that my usual social companion, Mary, wasn't with me—and I'm not the type to make social calls uninvited—Jack hid his surprise. He made me welcome and offered a seat in one of the lawn chairs in the yard.

We sat next to each other, and the Lab settled down at his feet. He pulled out a tobacco pouch and some papers and asked me if I wanted a smoke.

"No thanks, Jack, I finally whipped it."

"Go ahead. Right-on man, more power to you," he said.

"It's about the hundredth try, but I think I'm gonna make it stick this time."

"Well if ya ain't smokin' tobacco, we could share some wacky weed."

I'm not really a smoker in that sense, but if you're going to smoke pot, sitting in the middle of a two hundred acre forest with a trusted friend is the best, most relaxed and thoroughly right place to do it.

"OK, roll one, and I'll toke it with you," I said.

Jack pulled a baggie out of another pocket, filled a cigarette paper, rolled it with practiced fingers, licked the seal on the paper and handed me the "J." He flicked a butane lighter and held a flame to the tip of the joint. We traded it back and forth until the roach was too small to handle; then he dropped it on the ground and stubbed it out with his boot.

The pot relaxed me.

"How's Mary and them girls?" he asked.

I knew he was curious about my visit so I decided to show my hand.

"Well, we had to send Julia off to the desert to try to get control of her, and I'm not feeling too good about it."

"So what's with Julia? She's a great kid, didn't know there was problems."

"Yeah, she started high school this year, and some older guys got hold of her and things haven't been goin' so well."

"What? The kid's fourteen, what older guys?"

"Some asshole by the name of Mike has been taking advantage of her and gotten in between Julia and me and her mom. I mean, she thinks he's her family, sorta."

"That's bullshit."

"I think this guy's been doin' this to other girls too. He needs to be stopped."

"You plannin' on doin' somethin' about that?"

"I know where he lives, and I'm thinking of paying the boy a visit."

"What's Mary think of that?"

"Oh, Mary can't know. She would *not* be on-board. She's doesn't seem to care about who did this to Julia. All she can think about is getting Julia straightened out. Right now, she's happy to have Julia at camp. They were at each other's throats over the stuff Julia was doing. She's relieved to have a break from the constant confrontations. I don't want to get her worrying about this little detail."

"I won't say nothin'."

"Thanks, Jack. I can't get it out of my head that this guy needs some counseling, and I'm thinking it's time he and I had a 'come-to-Jesus meetin'."

"You needin' any help with that?"

"Yeah, Jack, I need a favor."

"Done."

***

That night I fell asleep mulling over our plan. Around midnight, I slipped out of bed. Mary stirred a little, interrupting her gentle lady-snore but didn't wake. I dressed in silence by moonlight from the window. When the backdoor hinge squealed, I stopped and held my breath, but it didn't raise an alarm, so I closed the door without a sound and went directly to the barn. I picked up a hiking backpack, stuffed it with a roll of tape and a can of spray paint from the workbench, grabbed the softball bat, and let gravity roll the car down the driveway until it was far from the house before I started the motor.

Jack met me at the old mill lot at the south end of town, and we transferred my stuff into the bed of his pickup.

Five-sixty Plum Street was one of those fifties-era houses, all built on the same floor plan by cocky ex-G.I.s in their twenties who felt immortal after being blessed with the dumb luck of surviving the war. Three bedrooms shared a short hall. One big one for mom and dad, a small one for the boys, and a little bit larger one for the girls. Everybody took turns at the one bath. The house reminded me of my childhood and growing up in one like it.

We sat in the truck observing the house. Heavy draperies covered the front picture window. Some yellowish light bloomed from a decorator window set artistically askew in the maple front door, probably the hallmark of some by-gone builder. The paint on the south side was peeling off in sheets. The window sills were bare wood. Rusted-out gutters dripped remnants of the evening shower, and tall grass in the front yard finished the picture of abandonment. I knew he was in there. The little shit-head.

Violence is anathema to me. I avoid it, despise it, and disavow it. This was different. I knew for certain Julia wouldn't testify against this guy. She thinks he's "mister wonderful" and would see him as a victim if I tried to have him prosecuted. She probably thinks they're in love.

Love—oh boy, there's a black hole, rocket to the moon, or tumble into nirvana—whatever open-ended infinite metaphor says it for you. It's the best part of what makes us human. I would never deny anyone the opportunity to enjoy it when it's real. The problem comes when a villainous schemer fakes it to seize control of another. No one is immune. Anyone could come under the spell of a master of manipulation. I knew without question that Julia would take his side. At fourteen, she lived on hormones and emotion. Her monthly period seemed to be lasting two years. It worked for him and against me.

No legal action could prevent him from getting away with what he'd done. I'm sure he knew it and counted on it. But, I did feel an obligation to stop him from doing more. I had pulled Julia out of it, so I can't say I was doing this for her sake. I tried to be honest with myself, but I couldn't figure out if my real purpose sought justice or revenge.

Did I usurp the authority of judge and jury, trying to make myself feel better by punishing this kid for making a mess of my once happy family?

If I aimed to bring him to justice, there could be no doubt this guy deserved some. If I wanted vengeance and retribution, could anyone blame me? He preyed on innocent girls. Julia's diary entries documented his routine. He took them down one at a time with a formula. He had looks and a worldly attitude that attracted and fooled them. He was cool. He had drugs and liquor. He was the anti-parent. He treated them like they were adults—or so they thought. The girls never knew what happened until he kicked them aside and moved on to the next one. The guy was good at it, that's for sure.

I looked at the damage he'd done to my family. There were many pages of evidence in Julia's diary that confirmed him as the one who set my daughter against us. He introduced her to sex and drugs at the age of fourteen and derailed her schooling. Until then, Julia had been an honor student.

Violence was going to happen here. I had to keep it under control. I had to keep Jack under control.

"Ya'll ready for this?" Jack said with a hand on my shoulder. His question hinted that he was a little unsure of my commitment. We both knew I was way the hell out of my element.

"Let's do it," I said, hoping my false bravado wasn't too obvious.

We pulled on black ski masks. Jack grabbed the bat out of the pick-up bed, a signal to me he was taking the lead. I carried a roll of duct tape and a can of spray paint. At the top of the front steps, he stood back—judged the distance to the door—gave me a nod that charged my confidence and raised his right knee waist high in front of him. When he shot the heel of his boot hard at the knob, the doorjamb splintered. The door swung wide open and banged against the inside wall. In a second we were standing in the middle of a small living room.

"Don't move a lick, any a' you," he shouted and brought the bat down square in the middle of a glass-top coffee table to the sound of shattering glass and cracking wood. I cringed and kicked the door shut behind us.

"First person moves is going to taste the end of this bat, got it?"

Four faces looked up at us in shocked disbelief. Two big guys wearing ski masks filled the small room. There were couches on either side of the destroyed coffee table. A boy and girl sat on each one.

The boys were in their late teens or early twenties. The girls looked like pre-teens to me, but they were probably right around Julia's age, thirteen or fourteen. All four had a stoned look, like they were sixty seconds behind current reality. Some had been drinking from the looks of the bottle and can trash on the floor, and the smell of stale beer.

"Who the hell are you?" shouted the braver of the two boys.

"Shut the fuck up, asshole" Jack said. He swung the bat past the guy's face, missing his nose by inches and smashing the table lamp next to him. The kid was forced to roll back on the couch. Sparks flew, and the light went out. "I'll do all the talking here; you fuckers better listen to me real good." The other guy wasn't quite so bold and sat frozen in place. With the lamp smashed, the only light in the room came from a dim bulb ten feet down the hall casting long shadows on the floor and walls, painting silhouette-duplicates of everyone in the room and giving the whole scene an unreal eerie aura.

"You two girls git down the hall into one a' them bedrooms and don't come out here again until we're gone," Jack said. "We have a few things to say to your boyfriends here. Go! Git down the hall."

The two girls looked anxious to put some distance between them and us, so they did as they were told.

"Now you two pricks are going to get some education. You need to sit quietly while we give you instruction on how to behave like honorable men when you grow up—if you ever do," Jack said.

I tore a long strip off the roll of duct tape and wrapped mouthy boy's wrists together behind his back. The lamp smashing bat swing had forced some respect into him. I had a feeling this was the Mike of the diary, and I had no desire to listen to any of his bullshit.

"Hey, where do you come off..."

Jack cutoff Mike's sentence with an open hand slap to his cheek which blossomed into a rosy glow.

"What's it you don't understand about 'shut the fuck up,' shit for brains? We'll do all the talkin' here, you two'l do all the list'nin'. Now keep your mouth shut or we can do some more talkin' and slappin'. It's all up to you pal." Jack's vocabulary wasn't very expansive, but he did have a way with words.

When Mike's hands were wrapped, I taped his ankles together. Then it was the other guy's turn, and we had both of them sitting immobile on the couches.

I had prepared a lecture for them.

"I am here to provide you guys with a lesson in moral values and statutory law which you should have gotten from your fathers. We are going to talk about using underage girls for sex and what the consequences might be for a male over the age of eighteen who can't keep his dick in his pants. According to the laws of the state of Oregon, no person under the age of eighteen is capable of consenting to a sexual act. Therefore, if you do have sex with them, you raped them. That's the law. Statutory rape gets you labeled as a sex offender. You may only serve a few years in prison, but you are going to be branded for life. Are you boys listening?"

My reluctant students sat quietly, looking down at their shoes.

"Now I know for a fact that you," I pointed my finger at Mike while Jack aimed the end of the baseball bat at him and poked him in the chest with it, "are guilty of statutory rape at least once."

"You don't know anything..." another slap shortened Mike's comment.

"An' you," Jack gave the other guy the bat in the chest treatment, "are prob'ly guilty too," Jack said.

"I'm not going to take you to court this time," I said. "And I'm not about to hear opposing arguments from you two sleaze bags, but from this moment on, there are going to be consequences if I find out you are ever doing this again."

"All this jawin' is makin' me thirsty," Jack said. "Let see if they's any beer left. Here, hold on to this." Jack handed me the bat, "I'll be right back."

I watched around the corner as he stepped into the kitchen, opened the refrigerator, and put a baggie in the freezer compartment. He grabbed a beer and returned to find the two struggling with their bindings.

Jack gave me an amused look and a nod that spurred me to action. I swung the bat overhead in a wide arc and smashed it onto the broken coffee table—I was starting to get the feel of the thing—and they stopped squirming. Jack grinned his approval and snapped open the beer can with his thumb nail. He took a long pull and handed it to me. It tasted good. I finished the can and tossed the empty through the hole in the coffee table.

"Ahhhh, that's better," I said. "So I think you guys know what I'm talking about, and I don't think you'll be boffing any freshman girls any more, but if you do get the itch, remember—this is a small town. I know who you are, and we can find you any time we want."

"Girls! Girls! I want you to come back in here right now," I said.

The two teens returned from down the hall. One of them was shaking. For a second I saw Julia there, but the crazy thought vanished.

"These guys are known rapists," I said. "I don't want you talking to them ever again. I want you to walk out the front door, go out to the sidewalk, turn right, and keep going. Don't turn back, don't look back, and if you don't want to be involved in a messy lawsuit, don't tell anyone you were here tonight. Now go!"

I opened the front door and the two left quickly. I watched from the door as they followed my instructions.

"I hope I never have to come back to see you guys again," I said. "Have a nice evening,"

"Later," Jack said and threw the bat on top of the coffee table mess.

With that we followed the girls out and closed the door behind us. I shook up a can of day-glow orange spray paint until it rattled, walked over to the doublewide garage and scrawled, "SEX OFFENDER" in 12 inch high letters on the door. Jack took the can over to the blue sedan in the driveway and wrote "RAPEST" in day glow on the driver side door. I didn't feel the need to correct him on the spelling.

We got in the truck and drove away. After a few blocks, I called 911 on my cell phone and reported a break-in at 560 Plum Street.

"What was in the bag you put in the freezer, Jack?" I asked.

"A little present for the boys. They had a hard night so I left them some cocaine and methamphetamine."

I made another call to the 911 operator. "Just so you know, there might be some drugs in the freezer, and they belong to a guy named Mike."

A few blocks later, two city police cars with red lights flashing and sirens whining passed us going the other way.

***

I woke the next morning with a disquieting anxiety, uneasy about the consequences of what I'd done. I stared wide-eyed at the ceiling while my head cleared, and I came completely out of the dream. It shocked me to realize where my psyche had taken me and what my pent-up anger could cause me to contemplate. There was a certain pleasure in the adventure, but that was overwhelmed by the discomforting knowledge that those boys could stir me to violate my most important principles and values. If I did any of the acts in the dream, I would forever be a different person. I couldn't let that happen. I could never give them that power.

With a sigh of relief, I called Jack and told him the whole thing was off. I sensed his disappointment in me, but he assured me he was ready to go if I changed my mind.

Agonizing emotions
Wandering thoughts
Intense realizations
The ache never stops.
Constant tortures
Of mind and soul
Settling my head
Will be my goal.

CHAPTER 14

JULIA

After a couple weeks, I begin to calm down. I get more used to the routines. The hikes are hard, but I look forward to the day when they'll get easier. I really like the group sessions when we all come together as a family-type thing. They make me feel more comfortable, not so alone. I'm getting used to the people; they're all interesting and so different, yet the same. I love that about them. It's weird, even the food tastes better.

I made up with Katie yesterday. She slipped and fell on the trail right in front of me. She looked like a stranded turtle lying there face up on top of her backpack, waving her arms and legs. I wrinkled my face to hide my smile and gave her a hand to help her up. We didn't say anything about the fight, but she said "Thanks" when I got her back on her feet. The way she said it told me we're gonna be OK.

I'm beginning to change my view of being here. I feel more of it being for my benefit than I did before. I'm finding all these things inside me that I knew were there but never got to come out, like I never took the time to look at them. I'm starting to admit my weaknesses more than I used to. It was like, if I didn't admit to them, they weren't there or would disappear. Things are weird like that. I keep thinking about my friends, and what they're doing and what I could be doing, but I think—oh well—I have the rest of my life to do nothing or "normal things." I see it as an experience. It all still seems like a dream, and I still want to be home, but more and more I'm coming to terms with stuff.

I like writing stuff down in my journal like this. It's a lot easier to write stuff down than say it, but I always want to find a way to express myself. I think sometimes I do things that are wrong, just to prove I'm different.

Well, I finally got my rules down to the point I can recite them like a moron. They made a big deal about giving me a real pack with a frame and everything. I couldn't get my stuff moved into it fast enough. I'm so tired of looking through a total jumble every time I want anything. There are pockets and zippers all over the thing. It makes the hikes a lot easier, but the last hike was still hard—I just can't see how I can do that all the time. I try to keep a positive attitude, but it's getting tough. I get really frustrated with some things. The weather is really starting to bother me, it's so finicky.

I keep having bad dreams about not being able to see my parents and bad stuff happening. I still wish I was home. I guess it has gotten a little easier, but not much. I can't wait to get another letter from my parents. I never thought I'd miss them this much. OK, I have to admit it—I didn't appreciate them before. I hate knowing that I put myself here. My fear is that I can't do all the stuff to graduate. Everything is so hard, and I'm scared that every wrong thing I do puts me here for another day or something. I want to do well, but I'm scared I might fail. What if I can never bow drill a fire? What if I can't make these hikes? What if they don't let me graduate?

I almost feel like this isn't really happening—I'm in some weird movie—but it is, and I can't stop it. I'm not used to being in situations that are so final and so strict. It scares me to see all these people who have been here for so long. I can't even imagine what it's like for them, and it makes the reality of my being here even more awful. I think that might be part of my problem. I don't like reality, so I try to work around it 'till I can't avoid it, and it hits me in the face. I miss my friends too. I know some of them are bad or have problems, but I love them all the same. I don't think my parents will ever understand that.

CHAPTER 15

BREE

Darla never does organize an A team. She tries to get her stooges to harass me like they did Julia, but I ignore them. The nice thing about not having any friends is you don't have to worry about losing them. It really made her mad when I didn't cave in. There's something about having a true enemy that makes me feel mature in a funny satisfying way. Like, I know enough not to be fooled by her, and I'm smart enough not to let her bother me.

So now what? Communication by letter only, someplace in the east Oregon desert, unclear when she comes back. This is my sister we're talking about. We have never even been separated for more than a couple of days before all this started. She is absolutely the closest thing I have to a real friend. Sure, we fought lots of fights and argued about things and space. But the little brat wouldn't give up sleeping with me until she was eleven years old. They would put her in her bed, and she would climb right out to get under the covers with me and fall asleep.

"Don't touch me," I would tell her. "You can be in here if you want to, but don't touch me."

She had to touch me to fall asleep.

"OK, you can touch me with one finger and that's all." She would poke out her index finger and touch my shoulder, and we would fall asleep together like that every night.

So now she's out in the desert, alone, with no one to touch. The best I can do is write to her. I'll write. The rules are pretty simple. I can write to Julia as much as I want and get letters back from her. My letters can cover anything I want, but—I can't pass on letters from any of her friends, and I can't pass any messages from her friends in my letters. It makes the letter writing kind of tedious, but I decide to follow the rules if it will help her. I still get one out every week. I try to make them happy and joking because I know Julia will be wanting a smile once in a while. She's got a good sense of humor, and I hope I can get her to see some humor in this situation.

I keep getting letters that the "friends" want me to send to her. Those are flushed immediately in the last stall in the downstairs girl's room when I have my morning break. I never even read them myself. When they ask why the letters aren't answered, I tell them I don't know, probably the camp censor and leave with a smile on my lips.

I get a few letters back from Jules, but mostly she addresses her letters to the three of us. The letters she writes back talk about missing me and her friends and asking about our household dogs and cats. She sounds OK, like she's adapting and determined to get through this. I really miss the little brat. I love reading her letters.

Dear Bree,

Hey baby what are you up to? I am currently learning to bow drill a fire! Oh yeah! It's actually kind of fun but really hard. I haven't gotten any fires yet, but I will. If I do, I can move up to advanced and be home in thirty days. Gosh, it's a long time. I'm writing on my sixteenth day here. I miss home so much. We get a "shower" once a week; yuck, I feel dirty! There's one girl counselor, Amy, who's pretty cool. I feel like she cares about us. We get to talk sometimes. The food is horrible. We have beans one night, rice and lentils the next, and that's it, it keeps alternating. For breakfast, we alternate ten grain— which is literally chicken feed—with oatmeal. We hardly ever get lunch, and if we do, it's instant mash potatoes or stuffing. Once a week we get fruit; it sucks. I am going crazy for real food (and candy). If you want, you can write and send me some "Airheads" or something flat that you couldn't tell was in the letter (hint, hint). I am trying to write you a not depressing letter full of sadness, but it is hard! I love you so much. W/B and tell me what's going on.

Always and forever, your one and only sister, Julia

Irreverently voluble voices
An incessantly uncanny
Train of thought
Immaculate reputations
That were thoroughly
Touched up.

CHAPTER 16

JULIA

Mark tells us we're staying in camp the next day. It means we'll have a little extra time to ourselves after dinner and probably see the therapist guy tomorrow. After dinner, I clean my cup, then pull the letters out of my pack, and go a little way back down the trail that we came in on. I feel Amy watching me as I walk away, but she doesn't say anything. I sit on a downed tree by the trail. It's about as private as I'm going to get. It feels good to be alone for a minute after being with the troop all day on the trail. I tear open all three envelopes and stack the letters in a pile. They're all from my dad.

Sunday, April 16

Dear Jules

It's Sunday morning and I woke up thinking about you as usual. We're having a lot of rain here so I imagine you are too and I hope you are able to stay warm and dry.

The more we learn about what has been going on in your life, the more we are certain we did the right thing in sending you there. I hope you are able to understand this and you're feeling less hostile toward us and can see how we didn't have a lot of options…

As expected. The first thing he tries to do is ease his damn conscience for what he did to me. Well, if it makes him feel better, fine, but he isn't going to convince me he had to do it. Shit, how many millions of kids grow up without being sent to Siberia? What the hell? He wants sympathy from me. No way. The second letter is worse.

> ...and you are a wonderful person and we know that. But your actions of late have not been wonderful at all. We couldn't stand by and do nothing. I came to understand we were hearing a cry for help and we didn't know how to help you anymore. The people you are with now do know how to help you. They don't know you as well as we do, but they can help you work through whatever has been bothering you.

Oh yeah, I'm so goddamn wonderful you sent me to desert hell with a bunch of Nazis who want to teach me how to be even more wonderful. This is what I expected from him. He's so straight laced and by-the-book. He probably never had any fun in his whole life ever. I wasn't fucking crying for any help. He's the one that can't handle it and has to hire these apes to do his dirty work for him. Power—it's all about who has power over who. Who can tell who, what to do, and when to do it. I don't need this, and I don't need them. I can take care of myself. When are they going to let go? Oh god, there's one more.

> ...so think about what has been going on in your life lately. Stand back and look at everything from an objective viewpoint and maybe you will get some idea of our point of view too. What if you were us? What would you be thinking about your daughter? What would you be doing about it? How would you feel if you were a parent and your daughter was saying and doing these things? What would you do? If you are ready to write us, I hope you'll respond to me with your thoughts and ideas about what has been happening. Think about it...

What's to think about? He still thinks I'm his baby. I know I'm not. End of thinking. How the hell am I supposed to know what I would do about my daughter? I'm fourteen. I don't have a daughter. When are they going to get real?

...We know a lot about what you have been doing in regards to sex and drugs, so don't feel you're revealing anything we don't already know if you want to discuss these things in your letters. The more we can get these things out in the open and talk (write) about them, the better. We want to deal with them in a positive way...

Oh great, they found my diary. Nothing's sacred with them. I have zero privacy. Who did they tell about all this? I can hear my mom blabbing everything to her old lady friends while they gasp in horror at my shocking immorality. Am I going to be the girl everybody whispers about when I walk by? I can't believe they're doing this to me. Have fun ladies, and when did he become an expert Freud?

...as I have been telling you all along, it is not our desire or intent to punish you, we only want to help you work through these things and get you back in control. We don't want to control you; we want to help you control you...

Well, if he doesn't want to punish me, he never should have sent me here and left me the hell alone. I wonder if he has any idea about what I'm going through. If he didn't want to control me, why is my every move programmed from the time I wake up until the time I get in bed?

I look up from the last letter to see Kevin staring at me. I know what he wants. I hand him the whole stack.

"Here, have a blast," I say.

"Wow, thanks Julia. Can I have them?"

"No, you read them right here, then I'm going to burn them in the fire pit."

"OK," he says. Kevin sits down on the tree next to me and starts reading.

"Hey, these are all from your dad. Doesn't your mom ever write you?"

"No, she's not much of a writer. She probably told my dad what she wanted him to say."

"Boy, these letters sound like they really care about you."

"Yeah, they sound like that."

"I got a letter from my mom when I first got out here, but my dad never wrote me," Kevin says.

"Did you write them back?"

"No, I didn't know what to say. Are you going to write back?"

"Yeah, you bet I am. I have a lot to say."

Kevin goes quiet for a while and finishes reading. He pages through the three letters slowly, then hands them back to me.

"Can I see the letter you write back before you send it?"

"No, it's personal."

"I was thinking I might get some ideas from it to write to my parents."

"Oh. Look, if you want, I'll help you write one later. Right now I think I'm going to write mine."

"OK," Kevin says and sits there.

"Well you'll have to leave now and give me some privacy, OK?"

Kevin gets up and picks up a stick and waves it at me. "I'll go, but you promise to help me later."

"Yes, now go."

I'm not too excited about the letter chore myself, but I feel the need to state my case. I fold the three letters up and stick them into one of the envelopes. I walk back over to the fire pit and watch the other two envelopes burst into flame. Amy gives me paper and a pen. I write a paragraph, but decide it's too nasty and throw it in the fire. Then I take a little walk and start again.

Dear Mom and Dad,

From your letters I see you are in shock and looking for every possible answer to your questions. I looked at your list of all the things you think could have made me do all the things I did. I actually have an answer to the question, but first of all I'd like to say—music? That is the most ridiculous thing I have ever heard. Anyway my answer is that it was a combination of things, but they were all internal things. One would have to know my beliefs, what I believe life to be, what means what, why things are the way they are sometimes. Soon I will explain in better detail exactly what my beliefs are. I would like you to know my beliefs are changing and more open now. Another reason is plain curiosity; I was experimenting and having fun. These are the main things. You guys look too much into stuff. Sometimes things are what they are. One fact I would like to stress is I am a strong person. I never got into any trouble I wasn't "looking for," so to speak.

Example: I wasn't sweet talked by Mike at all (I would love to know who told you this). What happened, happened. I don't care anymore. It doesn't bother me and while we are on the subject; I got into situations willingly with my eyes wide open. Why? I don't really know. To me, it happened and it wasn't a big deal. People over-rate sex, if you're safe (which I was) it's not fun, it just is. The older guys I guess, because I was sick of immature little idiots. I don't know, it wasn't planned either. Drugs were an escape from reality; they were fun. I skipped school because I could, there isn't any huge long story behind it; it is. That's the best I can explain. I hope you realize my thoughts have changed, but this is how it was.

Always, Jules

PS. I hope this makes some sense.

A battle between
My mind and heart
My mind makes for
A better start
My heart aches
For a better day
I will find peace
It will come to stay

CHAPTER 17

JULIA

When the time comes for me to meet with this therapist guy, I figure it can't make things any worse than they already are, and maybe I'll be able to use him to get out of here—anything to get a break from all the hiking and camp-making crap. My plan is to tell him what he wants to hear, let him think I'm scared straight, and get him to tell these jerks I'm fixed so they feel like they've done their job and can send me back home—back to my friends.

"I'm Dr. David Miller," he says and sticks out his hand like I'm supposed to be his buddy or something. When I don't take it, he acts like he doesn't care and shrugs his shoulders and smiles. It isn't the "I know all about you and I'm going to straighten you out," preacher smile I'm expecting. It isn't a big toothy one either, considering the way his white mustache and beard kind of cover his lips where the words slip out of a furry round hole under his sunburnt nose. It's more of a bright, blue-eyed smile that says, "OK, I see we'll need to get to know each other first." I don't smile back. I want him to know I'm not going to be easy to push around.

"I'm Julia. I don't want anything from you except to get me out of here as soon as possible so I can get back home. If you can't help me do that, you're wasting your time."

"Look, Julia, I don't know what they told you, but I'm not a magician. I can help you through this if you want to talk, privately, you and me. I *am* a psychologist. I'm kinda like a priest or a doctor, so whatever we talk about is between you and me and nobody else. Do you understand?"

Why does everybody have to treat me like a moron?

Do you understand? Jesus.

"Well I don't like the way they treat me, and I don't think it's legal for them to keep me here against my will."

"Whoa up there, I'm not your advocate either. I'm not going to go to bat for you and intercede with the crew for you. That's not my job. You can tell me your complaints if you want, but I'm more interested in how you're feeling about the bigger picture of life and family—where you've been and where you're going."

We sit facing each other in camp chairs, a good ways off from the rest of the group. There's something about him I can't put my finger on, but I feel it right away. He's real, sorta like my mom—no cover. He has a kind of jolly friendliness about him. I mean with all that white hair and beard, and being sort of heavy set, all he needs is a red suit and a pipe with curling smoke and the picture would be complete.

"So, I'm here to listen to you Julia. Ever had anybody tell you they were ready to hear you out before?"

"Oh great, you're going to psycho me, and I'm gonna see the light. Is that it?" I ask.

"Look, I'm not going to bullshit you. I can't do anything for you. You have to do it for yourself. Sometimes people do things that don't make sense because they're bothered by something, and they don't know what or why—or maybe they have feelings they don't understand—or they're faced with situations they aren't prepared to handle—or who knows what?"

I can't believe my eyes when he pulls out a stub pipe and tobacco pouch, fills the pipe, and lights it with a wooden match he strikes off the arm of his chair. "Why should I talk to you? I don't know you from Adam. How do I know you're even what you say you are? You could be a nosey pervert for all I know."

"OK, fair enough, here's my credential." He pulls a thin leather wallet out of his pocket and flashes an official looking card at me. "I'm a registered psychologist with the State of Oregon."

I lean over for a good look. He hands it to me. He was a lot younger in the picture, and it gives his name as Dr. David Miller followed by Ph.D and a bunch of other letters. It has a gold embossed seal; it looks pretty official. It kinda lets the air out of my sails.

He watches me as I examine his license. He draws on the pipe and sucks the match flame into the bowl. White smoke fills the air with the musty sweet aroma of pipe tobacco. I give the wallet back.

"Satisfied?"

"OK, so you have a license to pile it higher and deeper. I don't want you poking around in my head."

"All I can do is listen to you. It gives you a way to sort it out for yourself. There is no test here. No right answer. You can tell me anything you want. Remember, it will be between you and me. I won't tell your parents. I won't tell the crew. I won't tell you if I think it's right or wrong. You can ask my opinion if you want, and I'll give it, but that's up to you. My opinion doesn't really matter; it's how *you* think about things that matters."

It feels a little weird to be talking like this in the middle of the scrubby desert with St. Nicolas, but it does feel good to have somebody to talk to that isn't giving me orders and bossing me around for a change. The deep quiet tones in his voice relax me a little, and a physical calm creeps up my tired legs and loosens the knot in my stomach. I let the full weight of my body sag into the chair. Some of my anger dissolves with the tension, but I'm not going to let this guy off easy, so I keep up the resistance. It's kind of a game then.

"Well, I already told you I don't like the way I'm being treated, and I think it's illegal, and as far as I'm concerned, you're an accomplice to a kidnapping, and you all ought to go to jail. I have rights, and these assholes are treating me like a two-year-old thumb-sucking kid."

"So why do you think they're treating you this way? How do you want to be treated?"

"I don't want to be treated like a child. I don't want to be told what to do every minute of the day. That's what my parents do. 'Where you going? Who you going with? Did you do your homework? Clean your room. Watch your language.' I'm not a damn moron. I can take care of myself. I know what I'm doing. I want out of here."

"What would you do if you could get out of here right now? Where would you go?"

I'd go back to my friends. They don't treat me like this. They understand me."

"And what would you and your friends do?"

"Well, I don't know, hang out. We smoke some pot, but that's not all that bad. My parents smoke pot."

"What else would you do?"

"What do you mean?"

"Well, is that all you would do? Hang out with your friends and smoke pot?"

"No."

"What then?"

"You're trying to trap me."

"No I'm not Julia. I'm trying to help you think about what you are doing. Let's think about how it would be if you lived with your friends and nobody interfered. How would that look?"

"OK, we would get jobs and share a house, I guess."

"What kind of job would you want?"

"I don't know. I could be a waitress."

"Have you ever been a waitress?"

"No, but how hard can it be to take orders and clean tables?"

"Well, I'm sure you're capable."

"See, there you go, making fun of me, 'I'm sure you're capable.' I don't need any shit from you. Keep you're sarcastic bullshit to yourself or we're through."

"Maybe we'll come back to this idea. We're still getting to know each other, so let me ask you how you feel about school."

"It's stupid."

"Anything else?"

"I don't need to know any of the crap they're teaching. I can read, write, add and subtract. What else do I need to know? And the teachers are like everybody else, 'Do this, do that. Where is your work? Why didn't you do it on time? Don't talk in class. Why are you late?' It's all a bunch of control freak bullshit. I don't need any of it."

"That depends on what you want to do in life."

"What is that supposed to mean?"

"Well, what do you want to do in life?"

"I don't know."

"Have you ever thought about it? What do you like to do?"

"I like to dance."

"What kind of dance?"

"Ballet. I like ballet."

"Were you studying dance before you came here?"

"No."

"Why not?"

"I don't know. I'm getting tired of all your questions. How much longer are we going to do this?"

"I think that's enough for today, but I want you to think about a couple of things to talk about when we meet again. Really think about what it would be like to live full time with your friends. Think about why you haven't been dancing. Picture yourself working as a waitress. See if there aren't other things besides these, you would like to do with your life."

He sticks out that big paw of his again. I stick my hands in my pants pockets and look at the ground until he takes it back.

"Think about it, Julia, I'll see you again next week. I'll look forward to it."

He stands up, kicks a pit in the dirt next to a rock by his chair with the toe of his shoe. He bends down and knocks the side of his pipe on the rock, and a smoking tobacco coal falls out into the hole. He kicks dirt over it and steps on it.

"See you doctor —uh?"

"David," he says. "Call me David. It's easy to remember if you think of Michelangelo's David—and how little we resemble each other." He gives a little laugh and walks away, leaving me sitting there across from his empty chair.

After walking a few steps, he turns and walks backwards as he shouts back to me. "Oh, and Julia, don't think you can get through this by telling me what I want to hear. It's been tried and doesn't work. You really need to be honest with yourself. Think about how you got into this situation." He waves and smiles, then turns back toward the camp.

CHAPTER 18

STEVEN

When Julia was little, she was loving and fun. I thought we had a good father-daughter relationship, but she changed—and we didn't notice. Mary and I had tried to be open with the girls. We expected them to find their own way. We didn't want to push them but offered a helping hand when they asked for it.

The wilderness experience philosophy was the opposite of ours. I read all of Edelman's books, attended his lectures. He told us we could not be effective parents *and* be our child's friend at the same time. I had a hard time with that.

I saw this episode as putting Julia on a temporary side trip that would take her back to the mainstream later, when the boat was ready for deeper water and the captain had regained control of the ship. For me, it was like jumping in to save a guy who'd gone off a bridge. You took a chance, and maybe the guy didn't want to be saved at the time, but you hoped with some dry clothes and a different frame of mind, he'd be thankful you saved him. That was my hope, that eventually she'd be grateful.

I felt a steady stream of letters to Julia would prevent her from feeling completely abandoned. I resolved to send at least two letters every week so there was always something from home whenever there was a mail call out on the trail. It made me feel a little more comfortable with what I'd done and a little less heart-broken when I thought of her being out there all alone. It felt cumbersome at first, but I soon realized, without the letters, we would be completely isolated from each other; so I wrote.

It helped me to get letters back from Julia too. One letter I will never forget. I could see words smeared on the page where two teardrops fell as she wrote. These weren't teardrops that come from a child's skinned knee or an accidental knock or cut. Oh no, these were the kind that come from a sad heart that wants comforting. Their essence was sadness and loneliness, and they welled up from a tight chest, full of emotion. These were the kind that makes a father want to drop everything and run to his daughter, hold her and make everything all right. I so wanted to be there to catch the third drop. I can't count the number of times I re-read that letter before I wrote back.

Dear Julia,

Your last letter had some real content. Let me address your issues.

You say we're "in shock." Yes we are. At the age of fourteen (now fifteen) you are not able to go out into the world and begin an independent life. You don't have the education, the experience, the skills. Yes, you can survive by begging shelter and food from other people, or trading sex for food and shelter, but neither of those approaches has much of a future. So when you run away, what is it you have in mind? If we simply let you go on doing what you were doing, what would be the result? How did you envision yourself surviving? Did you think about any of these things? If you did, tell us your plan. If you didn't have a plan, you demonstrated that you are not ready to handle an independent life yet. That's not a judgment; it's a fact.

You feel we're looking for answers. Yes we are. If we can't understand what is happening to you, we can't help you. Do you agree you need help? Anyone who is writing in a diary about suicide needs help. Nobody can argue with that. You weren't communicating with us or going to school; you were hysterical; men were taking advantage of you; you were doing drugs. If I told you those things about another person, wouldn't you agree they need help? Julia, you are out of it now, safe and secure, but what happens when you come home? We need a future that's different from the one you were working on.

It's not the music, it's the words. The lyrics you were listening to talked about death, pain, suffering, and dying. Why that is appealing to you I don't know, but those words wouldn't have a detrimental effect on a stable person. You were not stable. You were lost and looking for a reason to make it OK that you couldn't handle life. You were trying to "escape from reality" as you said.

So what are your beliefs? You write that you have these beliefs about life, but you never say what they are. Tell us.

There is nothing wrong with experimentation and having fun—unless you make it your life. I have seen people make it their life. People who started "experimenting and having fun" in their early teens and now they are still doing the same drugs and sex things in their 30s, 40s and 50s and that's it. That's their life.

We were afraid you were headed in that direction. You blew off school so you could spend your time experimenting and having fun. You can experiment without dedicating your life to it. You keep saying that you have been in control. So please tell me what your plan was for your education.

You prefer men who go back to high schools to pick-up freshman girls instead of freshman guys who are trying to learn about life. You say the freshman guys are "immature idiots," but the men you chose are immature predators.

If you want to escape from reality, there is something wrong with your reality. Change it.

I can see that you would be unhappy with school. You weren't going to class, you weren't doing the work, you weren't learning anything. How could you possibly enjoy school? You couldn't be successful with your approach, so you made it easy on yourself by deciding that school is stupid and worthless. Once you decided that, with the support of your friends, you don't have to worry anymore about being successful. Then, since you know in your heart that school is not stupid and worthless, you take drugs to make it easier to live the lie. It works. You escape from reality for a while, but the drugs wear off—and you find yourself back to being unsuccessful. So you do more drugs. Pretty soon you would stay high and really escape from reality.

You say that your thoughts are changing. That sounds promising, but I don't know what it means because I don't know what you were thinking or how it has changed. Fill me in.

Julia, my impression of what I'm getting in your letters is the same thing we have been hearing from you for a year. "Leave me alone! I know what I'm doing, and everything will be fine."

That is denial of the real situation. You can deny any truth, but your denial won't change the reality.

You are going to have to admit there are people in this world you can learn from. Admit that and you will be on the road to recovery. Don't admit that, and you are doomed to live the rest of your life in a boring world that never changes.

There is nothing wrong with learning from others. It does not belittle you to admit you made a mistake and need some help to fix it. I'll admit I have made my mistakes, or you wouldn't be where you are right now.

We don't want to run your life. You have to make your life choices. But they have to be choices based on reality, not based on what you would like reality to be. Deal with reality, embrace reality, control your reality, work with it, and don't deny it.

That's about it for now.

I love you,   Your Papa

Sorrowful frowns and
Very sore feet.
Unhappy groans and
Muscles that ache
Destinations reached
It all turns around
With a good night's sleep.

CHAPTER 19

JULIA

Doctor David Miller eases out of his chair when he sees me winding through the scrub bush on my way to his open-air therapy clinic: two gaudy, plastic-webbed, folding chairs set off beyond earshot of camp. He can't be much of a therapist if he doesn't even have an office and has to drive all the way out here to find work. This is gonna be another waste of time.

"Good to see you again, Julia," he says and motions for me to take the other seat. His chair sways and makes a metallic squeak when he resettles his chubby bottom. "Everything going OK?" He glances up at me, then down at the manila folder open on his lap. He can't be all that interested in me if he has to look at his notes to remember me. I feel like I'm a job to him. He scribbles a note.

"No," I say. It's nice to sit in a chair instead of squatting on my feet on the ground or sitting on the sandy dirt.

"What's on your mind Julia?"

"What do you think? I want out of here."

"Anything else?"

I'm not in a mood to talk to him. It's hot. The sun is so high overhead we don't even cast a shadow. I cross my arms and stare off at the distant pines where a hawk circles, then closes its wings in a swift dive for lunch.

It's probably that cute little rabbit I saw when we hiked in. I hate the law of the jungle.

I decide I'll bitch for a while until he gets tired of it. "Yeah, I get these lecture letters from my dad all the time. What is it he wants from me?"

"What do you think he wants?"

Here we go again with question and answer time. "I think he wants a little robot who'll do what he says, when he says it, and doesn't have an original thought. He wants to control me like he did when I was a baby. He doesn't care I've grown up. He doesn't think I can do anything."

"Really? Why do you think that?"

"Every time I do something, he has to tell me that I'm doing it wrong or how I should be doing it this way—or stops me from doing it and takes over. I don't want to be like him. I'm me, not him. Why can't he leave me alone?"

"Do you think he has anything to teach you?"

"No," I say. "He only knows about old stuff. He's like an obsolete dinosaur."

Miller smiles when I say that. "He's not quite that old is he?" He says it like it's an inside joke, and you have to be there, in an old person's head I mean, to get it.

"Well, he has no appreciation for music, hardly ever laughs, and thinks about serious stuff all the time."

"Is he concerned about you?"

"If he had any concern about me, he wouldn't have put me here in brain-wash-your- kid-into-submission-land would he?"

"What has he done besides that to make you so angry toward him?"

"Well he's never around, always working on something at his office or doing things around the house. He never sits down and veges-out with us. He makes us feel embarrassed to be watching TV. He thinks it's stupid, and we're stupid for watching it."

"Do you think it's stupid?"

"Well yeah, it's stupid, but it's fun to watch stupid stuff sometimes. He needs to lighten up."

"Did he ever do anything good for you?"

"Yeah, when we were little, he used to have fun with us. Swing us at the park or take us to the drive-in movies and kid stuff like that. I don't know why he changed."

"Maybe you changed."

"Of course I did, I grew up."

"So how does that make things different?"

"I don't need somebody telling me what to do all the time. I can think for myself. I know what I'm doing. I can pump my own swing."

Miller punches the button on his ballpoint and starts scribbling again. I look up, and there's the hawk. He has something in his claws. It's brown and smaller than the rabbit. It has a thin hairless tail that's waving like crazy while the bird's huge wings flap as it lifts way up and turns toward the steep cliffs on the horizon.

"What about your mother, do you talk to her about these things?"

"She's even worse than he is. There's *no* privacy with her. She's always calling my friends and even talking to their parents about me. If she wants to make sure I don't have friends, she couldn't pick a better way to do it. I don't want her to even know who my friends are. She's on me every minute as soon as I walk in the door; that's why I didn't come home sometimes. I didn't want to have to explain everything to her."

"So you know all about sex?" Miller asks me.

"They sent you my diary, didn't they?"

"Yes."

"Did you have fun reading it?" I don't know whether to be pissed off or embarrassed. I'm starting to get over my parents having the damn diary, and now they're sending it out to everyone. It'll probably be on the bestseller shelf right next to that Jewish girl's.

"Look, Julia, I know it's personal, and you never meant it to be read by anyone else, but you have to understand that when you made your parents worried about your safety and the direction you were going, they did the right thing. It was their duty to make sure you were protected. It's a parent's job. So what do you know about sex?"

I can't believe I'm talking about sex with this guy. "What's to know. It's a simple human function, results in babies if you don't watch out. End of story."

"Any love involved in there?"

"Nah, that's for kids," I say and there he goes again with that stupid smile. "It's a way to get people to know each other, that's all. Sometimes they get close with sex and fall in love, but it's not a sure thing. Most of the time the sex thing wears off, and off they go."

"Is that how it was for you?"

"What do you mean, is that how it was?"

"Well did you fall in love with anybody after you had sex?"

"No, I guess not."

"Why not?"

"Nobody was all that interested in the other person. They wanted the sex part, then be left alone."

"And that was OK with you?"

"Look, Mike said he loved me before and after we had sex, so it wasn't all physical you know."

"What about the drugs?"

"What about it? Everybody does some drugs now and then. I didn't really get into it that much. Had lots of offers, but I can take it or leave it."

"What about the other boys you had sex with? Why'd you do that?"

"Sometimes Mike asked me to, you know as a favor to his friend because he was a virgin or something. I don't know, he asked me to do it for him, and I did it with the other guys."

"Did they pay him?"

"Fuck you!—you know what, I'm done talking to you." I stand up and start walking away. Miller doesn't move. "You can go fuck yourself." I turn around and come back to face him.

"You are just like my dad." I'm yelling in his face. "Twisting everything into something bad or nasty when you have no idea what you're talking about. The world doesn't go by rules you make. We are the next generation, and we aren't going to make all the stupid mistakes you people made. We're smarter, and we're going to do it right. So don't you go getting all holy about everything and painting me with your awful-person brush because I don't even care what the hell you think because it doesn't matter to me or anybody else with a brain in their head. So keep your smutty little comments to yourself and don't be looking down on me from your goddamn therapist pedestal because you are no better than me or anybody else. Get it?"

Nobody says anything for a while. I glare at him. He sits there with a blank face looking at me. I wait for him to blink; he doesn't blink.

"So don't you have anything to say," I ask him when I can't take the silence any longer. "You going to sit there with your statue face and look at me and not say anything?"

"OK. Sit down Julia," he says.

"You see, this is the problem. You're just like my dad, no emotion, you're like talking to a stone," I say. I feel flushed and walk a few feet away. I see some faces turned toward us at the camp. Dr. David Miller calls me back.

"We'll talk about something else. Sit down."

I stand looking down on him. I don't sit because he told me to.

"Let's talk about getting me the hell out of here, that's what I want to talk about."

"We're going to get you out of here, but you'll have to give it a little time. What would you like to have happen when you get home? What would you want to be different?"

"I only want to be left alone to take care of myself."

"Does that include getting yourself to school and attending classes every day?"

"OK, so I screwed up on that. It's no big thing."

"But it's your responsibility."

"OK—yes—I can do that. I can go to school and all that."

"Before you leave here, you're going to have to agree to a contract with your parents. That is going to be part of the contract."

"I'm sure it is," I say and slump back into the chair.

Dr. David Miller picks up his pen and makes notes in his folder.

***

The next day it's back to the trail. We rise at the usual ungodly hour to Mark yelling out a wake-up call, then he makes a round to each of us, giving orders to start the day. When he gets to Kevin, there's no response.

"Get up Kevin, we're hitting the trail in one hour."

Kevin doesn't move. He lies there in his sleeping bag face down. Mark shakes the bag to get his attention.

"Now, Kevin, let's go."

Still nothing.

Mark grabs a handful of sleeping bag and rolls Kevin over so he's face up. He doesn't respond and keeps his eyes closed. It's obvious he's awake.

"OK Kevin, if this is the way you want it, the others are going to have to do your work, but you are not going to stop us from moving today," Mark says.

The rest of us set about taking down the camp. Chastity and I work on the fire pit.

"I want it to look like nobody's been here." Mark says. "Bury the charcoal and the fire-scarred rocks. We are visitors to this land; it should look the same when we leave as it did when we came."

Everybody works except Kevin. He refuses to get out of his sleeping bag and won't respond to any questions. He lays there. He doesn't even open his eyes when Amy comes around with a bag of oranges. She tries to get him up, but he ignores her. Everybody grabs an orange like they're starving; it's powerful sweet after nothing but ten-grain. Jimmy D. is weirdly excited when he whispers to me, "We're gonna party."

I think, OK, these kids have been out here way too long if getting an orange feels like a party. Jimmy stuffs the orange carefully into his pack. Everyone else eats theirs immediately—except Kevin. I'm not sure, but I think Jimmy D. gets Kevin's.

When we finish breaking down the camp, I ask Chastity, "What's the deal with Kevin?"

"Hard to tell. He gets this way sometimes, and there's nothing anybody can do. He has to come out of it on his own." She shrugs her shoulders and starts to walk away.

"So what will they do, stay here until he decides to get up?" I say after her.

She turns back to me, brushes her yellow hair back with both hands, gives me a kinda knowing smile. "Oh no, you'll see, we're going whether he cooperates or not."

The rest of us do our part. When we're done, you really can't tell there's been a camp there at all, except for our light foot prints in the dust. It finally comes down to Kevin, who still hasn't moved.

Mark calls us together. "Everybody over here. Do you all have your personal packs ready to go?" We all nod. "Then we're going to have to make a carry for Kevin. Sam and Jimmy—find us a couple of strong poles, long enough to make a stretcher and stout enough to hold Kevin. Julia and Chastity, put Kevin's pack together and make it ready to leave. Katie, go with Amy to get some blankets for the stretcher sling. We are going to be on the trail in thirty minutes, MOVE!"

The boys come back with some madrone poles, and Mark knocks the branch stubs off with a hand axe. Amy brings a khaki wool blanket. Mark oversees the boys wrapping the blanket around the poles and lashing them up to make the stretcher. The boys roll Kevin onto the stretcher face up, sleeping bag and all. We shoulder our packs. With Jimmy D. and Sam at one end and Chastity and Katie at the other, they lift the stretcher to start down the trail.

"Kevin," Mark says. "You aren't pulling your weight. We are not going to let you stop the rest of us from making this hike. The sooner you pick yourself up and get going the better. If you have a reason for your behavior, tell us, and we'll see if we can help you. This puts you back to square one in your program. You are not getting any closer to going home when you act like this."

Kevin says nothing. He lies in the sling with his eyes closed. We trade-off carrying the stretcher. My arms ache from the weight of it. It doesn't bother the boys.

"Hey Kevin, why are you being such an asshole?" Sam says while he carries. "You think you're something special to make us carry you like this? We'll get you back for this you big baby." It doesn't faze the kid.

Jimmy D. bounces the stretcher up and down to mess with Kevin, but I make him stop because the jolting hurts my arms even more.

Chastity comes up alongside the stretcher and tries. "Kevin, we're all on your side; what is it? Talk to us so we can work out whatever is bothering you."

He doesn't respond to her either.

It's at least an hour before Mark calls for a break. Jimmy D. and Sam look at each other with smart-alec grins and drop their end of the stretcher with a thud that I think could knock Kevin out, but he still doesn't stir.

Amy comes over to Kevin for another try. "What is it Kevin? If there's a problem, let's get it out."

Kevin opens his eyes, pulls his right arm out of his sleeping bag, points a finger right at me, and says, "Ask her."

I look around at all the others and throw up my hands. I have no idea why I'm involved in the Kevin trouble.

"What are you talking about Kevin?" I ask.

Kevin sits up and turns to me. "You know—the letter."

"I let you read the letters, what do you want?"

"You said you'd help me write a letter, then you blew me off."

"No I didn't. I told you I'd help you and I will."

"When?"

"Whenever you want."

"Right now."

"No, Kevin, I'll help you tonight after dinner."

"How do I know?"

"Well, everybody here heard me promise, and I'll do it."

"And if she won't do it, I'll do it," says Chastity.

"No, I want her." Kevin says pointing at me again.

"I'll do it, Kevin," I say.

Kevin squirms out of his sleeping bag and gets up. He rolls it up and lashes it to his pack. Sam and Jimmy D. breakdown the stretcher. When we get back on the trail, Kevin leads the way.

My surprise at Kevin's insistence gets me to think about the letters. They haven't been that important to me, but I guess if I didn't get any, not getting them would be important. Kevin seems like such a baby to me. He's only a year younger, but he's so immature. I try to remember what it was like for me when I was younger like him, but I can't put myself there. It seems so many ages ago. Then I try to see if I can think like Kevin. What would it be like if my parents didn't send me any letters? I know my busybody parents wouldn't do that. What if they left me out here in the desert and didn't think about me at all and went on about their lives as if they didn't have a kid? My parents are probably talking about me right now, analyzing everything I did, planning my future for me. Well, Kevin has his parents, and I've got mine. I guess we're both stuck with what we've got, good or bad. Sometimes I wish my parents were like his, that they'd leave me alone, and I could run my own life. Other times, I don't think I would want to be completely forgotten and left entirely on my own. There are a few things I haven't learned yet. I'll do my best for Kevin. I'll help him write a good letter. Maybe we can get them to write back. I don't know.

***

After we set-up camp and eat dinner, I find Kevin sitting by the burned-out fire pit.

"C'mon, we'll sit under that tree and write your letter."

He brings out his journal for paper. He hasn't written much in it, but we fold it over to a fresh page and I hand him a pen.

"OK Kevin, now what do you want to write?"

"You write it, whatever you think."

He tries to hand the pen back, but I won't take it.

"No, this is your letter. It has to be in your handwriting, and it has to say what you want it to say."

"Well, how do I start?"

"Who are you writing to, your mom or dad or both?"

"Probably my mom, my dad would never write me. He's too busy."

"That's OK, you can write to both of them and see. Start out 'Dear Mom and Dad.' "

"Then what?"

"Tell them what you've been doing and how you feel."

"All right, but you'll still have to help me."

Dear Mom and Dad,

I know you didn't hear from me for a long time, but I have been busy here. I got a friend named Julia who is helping me write this letter. She's very pretty and nice.

Kevin looks up at me when he writes that.

"You got a crush on me, Kev?" I say.

"I like you and thanks for helping me," he says.

I know I embarrassed him so I change the subject. "OK, what else you gonna say?"

I hope you are doing fine. It seems like I been out here for a long time and wish you would write me a letter. Julia is getting lots of letters from her parents, and she lets me read them. I know you're busy and don't have much time to write, but maybe you could send a note or you could dictate one to your secretary.

Kevin

"That's good Kevin. Maybe you could sign it, 'Love Kevin.' They might like that."

"Yeah, that's good." Kevin scratches in the word.

We fold it up, write the envelope, and give it to Amy to mail.

"When do you think they'll get it?" Kevin asks.

"Three or four days I guess."

"Do you think they'll write back right away?"

"Probably."

"Good."

When Kevin smiles, I have to smile too. It's kinda like when one person yawns, you can't help it, and you yawn too. I guess we both feel good about his letter.

"You're sure they'll write back?" he says. The smile is gone.

"Not a doubt in my mind." I'm not about to burst his bubble. I hope it happens and soon for his sake. I think about writing my letter. Maybe I shouldn't be so mean to them. I decide to think about it.

***

We hike every day that week. Kevin stays with me on the trail. All of a sudden he wants to talk, and I let him. It makes me think about other stuff instead of brooding about myself. His deal is way different from mine. I mean his family is not what they call middle class. They have money, lots of it from what I get out of his telling me. He has an older sister that's out of college and studying in Spain to learn the language so she can be a diplomat. His older brother is a lawyer and works in Washington for a senator and hangs around the White House and stuff. His dad works on Wall Street in New York City, but Kevin can't tell me what he does there, only that he has a huge office on the top floor of a skyscraper and is always working and meeting people at night, usually with his mom. Kevin actually came to the desert from boarding school, that's sort of a orphanage for rich kids when their parents don't have time for them.

"Wow, Kev, sounds like you got it made," I say after listening to his story.

"You wouldn't say that if you were me. I don't have nobody to talk to. You're the first person that really listened to me my whole life."

"Well you can talk to the therapy guy, can't you?"

"He's all like everybody else, trying to get me to say things he wants me to say. That's not listening like you do."

I'm starting to feel a little proud of myself for being his muse, but I know better than to think I can do anything for him but listen.

"You know what, Kev, I got the same problem as you, maybe not so bad. I bet all the kids here have the same problem—parents that don't understand us."

"Yeah, they think we're supposed to follow them and be like them and do what they do and be happy with it, when we don't want any of it."

"Yeah, then they say, 'What is it you want?' like we're supposed to know what we want the day we're born or something. I don't know about you, but I want to find that out for myself—try stuff and see what works for me. Not be afraid to screw up once in awhile. Have some fun doin' it too."

"I think I want to be something that nobody else has ever been before," Kevin says. "You know, like find an alien race or invent an anti-gravity machine or be a human brain overhaul mechanic or discover a cure for war."

"Boy that would be something, a cure for war. Do that, Kev."

"You ever had sex?" he asks.

"Back off there, Kev—you and I are friends—OK?"

"No Julia, I only wanted to know if you did or not."

"OK, yes, I did."

"So what was it like?"

"That depends. Sometimes it was kind of icky with some guys, and sometimes it was a trip to heaven with other ones. I couldn't tell you why."

"So how do I get a girl to have sex with me?"

"Just be nice to her and be interested in her. It will happen. Don't worry, it's a natural thing, it will happen. But don't be a jerk and do it only for sex, if they think you really like them. You have to tell the truth, Kevin; we get hurt pretty easy if guys lie to us. But sometimes it *is* just for fun, and you gotta know the difference. You'll know, be honest with yourself, and you'll know. The problems start when one person thinks it's this and the other one thinks it's that."

"OK."

Mark comes down the line of hikers and tells us to stop talking. He makes me stand still to let Kevin get a little farther ahead of me, then walks back to the end of the line. When I'm sure he's way back, I catch up to Kevin again.

"Hey, what did you do that got you sent here, Kev?"

"Ran away from that stupid boarding school. It was OK there I guess, but not really. It happened."

"What happened?"

"Well, I wasn't planning it or anything, but they were making us read this book about this girl Jane Eyre. Her family put her in a orphanage because they didn't like her, and the people that ran the place were really mean to her."

"I hate it when they make us read that stuff."

"Yeah, it made me sad. I felt sorry for her, and then I felt sorry for myself. I kept thinking, why didn't she run away and get out of there? Then the idea came to me that I should run away. One night I got in bed with all my clothes on and waited until they put the lights out. They always locked us in at night, but I knew of a way out through the laundry chute.

When I got out of the building, it was dark—no moon. I climbed over the gate, and I stumbled out onto the road and put my head down and kept walking."

"I get you. I ran away too, Kev. Where'd you go?"

"By the time the sun started coming up, I was a few miles away from the school. I mean I walked the whole time and never stopped. It felt good and kinda scary, but once I got out of there, I couldn't turn around. I knew I had to get rid of my school tie and sweater, so I ditched them in some bushes and got off the road whenever anybody was close by. I was afraid to stay on the road after it was light, so when I came to a railroad track, I turned off and followed it, walking right down the middle between the tracks. When I got to a place where the tracks went over this old wooden bridge, I looked through all the crossed boards under me and saw some people down there around a fire. I was getting hungry by then, and I went down."

"Boy, you were brave."

"Not really, I was mainly hungry. I wasn't thinking about anything else. I was tired from all the walking and hungry. There was a bunch of old guys and a old woman down there. I mean they looked old and dirty, and the men had beards and wild hair."

"Weren't you scared?"

"After they saw me, I got a little scared because I didn't feel like I could run away anymore. Then this big guy got up from their camp fire and came up the hill to meet me coming down. 'What are you doin' here?' he said to me. I didn't know what to say. 'Who are you kid?' he asked me. I looked at him and the others, and froze.

"They had a small campfire going, and I saw some ragged sleeping bags and blankets lying around like they all slept there during the night. There were six or seven of them, and they were all looking at me. The woman came up behind the guy and pushed him aside and said, 'Come on kid, we'll get you a hot coffee and a little breakfast before, Looper, here gives you the third degree.' That made me feel better, and I came down off the hill and into their fire circle. When I sat down with them and got a close-up look, they all seemed pretty nice really.

"Looper kept asking me questions. 'You ran away from the school, didn't you?' He was the only one who cared one way or the other. I told them I was out for a walk and got lost. He didn't believe me. I could tell 'cause he kept up with the questions. 'Where do you think you're goin'? he asked.

"I said I wasn't going anywhere, only out for a walk. The woman handed me a cup with coffee. She told me her name was Mazy or something like that. I started getting nervous with all the questions and told them I needed to get going. The coffee made me feel better, but I was still nervous. Mazy gave me a sandwich. It was nothing but bacon between two slices of bread, but it was sure good right then. They kept after me with the questions. I was getting ready to tell them the truth when five policemen came runnin' down the hill with their guns in their hands and all, shouting 'Don't anybody move.' Boy, you should have seen those people disappear. One minute we were sittin' there, and the next I was all alone, surrounded by cops.

"They didn't chase the others. They came right for me. I knew the school sent 'em. They took me straight back there. I sat outside the dean's office and listened to him talking to my mom on the phone. He went on for a half hour, 'what do you want us to do?' and 'I'm sorry but we can't keep him' over and over again. Then he read her a phone number for somebody called Edelman, and he came out and told me to pack up. I've been here ever since."

"Guess we've all had our adventures with the police," I said. "What are you going to do when you get out of here?"

"I don't know. I can't go back to my parents; they're too busy. I guess they'll put me in another boarding school."

I don't know what to tell the kid at that point. I mean, it feels kinda hopeless to me. I know I'll be going back to my family. They'll be every bit as boring as before, but at least I know where I'm going and what to expect.

I see a grey squirrel run out from under a bush ahead of us as we walk along. There isn't much cover in the scrub brush, some sparse manzanita among the cedars. He dashes from one poor hiding place to another, kinda like Kevin—no destination, only running.

A tight round ball
All wound of twine
Emotional strings
Tears swell the knot
When troubles unwind
Oh—let them be kind!

CHAPTER 20

JULIA

Kevin's story makes me see my own situation a little differently. It takes me a couple of days to write a letter back to my parents. I finish it on one of our trail stops.

Dear Mom and Dad and Bree,

Well how are you guys? I just got all your mail at once a couple days ago. I wrote you another letter before this, but since have found more to say. You asked me to tell you about my days or describe it. I'll give you the whole schedule. We wake up at 7:30 or 8:00 (I don't really know because they never tell us). We have 5 minutes to get our stuff out of the shelter to our packs and all our stuff for breakfast at the fire pit. We cook it. Actually we write one goal and three objectives for the day, then cook it. We have forty-five minutes to eat and clean our mugs, which we clean with dirt by the way. Then we have twenty minutes for "hygiene" which consists of putting a little soap and water on a cloth and cleaning our face, feet and hands, then we brush our teeth. After this, on hiking days we "take down camp" (shelter, sump, latrine). Pack our packs. Tank a quart of water. Hike with our fifty pound packs anywhere from 3 to 6 miles to camp. Set up camp. Have dinner (same routine as breakfast), write in journals and go to bed. We do this five days a week. Two days we stay in one spot. Same breakfast and dinner thing except in the middle we actually have lunch on these days and we do our "laundry" and "take showers" and talk to our therapist and stuff. I guess that's our basic week anyway.

I like your letters and thank you so much for the poem Bree and the blister stuff. They wouldn't let me keep the brush, but thank you anyway! It has taken me awhile to write this letter. It is now May 2nd. I can't believe I will be spending my birthday without you. Yesterday I got to go into town for my physical. It is nice to know civilization is still there. You guys seem to be ignoring my question about Darla's and Maggie's address. I'd appreciate some feedback. I am at 21 days and most likely will be in "advanced" tomorrow or next Wednesday then thirty days till home! It is still so hard and I am so home-sick I hate it. I still just want to be home, but I'm doing my <u>best</u>.

Always, Julia

"You writin' a book or somethin'?" Jimmy D. says.
"A letter is all," I say.
We're stopped in a grove of pines. It's a shady relief from the mid-afternoon sun that makes the desert hills ripple in the hot air and creates cool-looking blue lake mirages on the flats. We each have our own tree to lean against so we would be a funny sight for someone who doesn't know us. Even the counselors are happy to be out of the sun for a while. Jimmy sits down next to me and drops his pack in front of him. He looks around at the others, then...
"Wanna get high?" he says in a whisper so quiet I almost don't get it.
I look at him. He reaches in his pack and pulls out a clear plastic water bottle bulging with a cloudy yellow-orange liquid. He looks around again, then whispers real close to my ear.
"Jailhouse gin, I made it from the orange and the sweet biscuit they gave us two weeks ago. It's aged over ten days."

He gives it a shake and twists open the cap. There's a whoosh of gas with a sweet-sour yeasty smell. Nobody else is close enough to smell it, but Mark turns to the sound. Jimmy D. clears his throat as a cover. Mark goes back to his book.

"Give me your cup, I hate to drink alone," he whispers.

I untie my cup from the leather strap on my pack and hand it to him. He gets his and splits the contents of the bottle between our two cups. I watch as a couple of fuzzy globs of yellow stuff go in with the liquid. He tips his cup slightly like a little toast, mouths "Cheers" and downs the whole thing. I smile at the face he makes. I throw mine back, swallowing the glob in the bottom, and choking down a cough as the liquid burns the back of my throat, then runs liquid fire through my chest and drops like a hot coal into my stomach.

The alcohol hits my brain a hammer blow. The fire in my throat makes me struggle for air, and I feel a warm rush go up my neck and into my cheeks. I must be making a face too because Jimmy laughs out loud. Everybody turns toward us.

"Very funny, Julia," he says. "She thinks she can convince Mark to let us stay here and camp tonight."

"Why not?" I say. "Come on, Mark, let's stay."

Mark and Amy confer.

"Not a bad idea," Mark says. "We're on schedule for the food drop at Windy City, and it's hotter than hell out there. But you all have to cooperate with an early start tomorrow and agree to push it hard and make up the miles we'll lose by not moving today."

Everyone agrees, and Mark gives the order to set up camp. My body feels limp, and I give a loud hiccup which makes the whole troop laugh at me—Jimmy especially. "Let's go," Jimmy says and gives me his hand to pull me up from the ground with a stupid grin on his face. I stand up on wobbly legs, then get my balance. Amy notices and asks if I'm OK.

"Yeah, I'm fine. My leg fell asleep, that's all," I say.

The world is spinning and my stomach feels queasy, but I pitch in with the camp set-up as best I can. It isn't until I get down some ten grain that I'm sure I won't puke. Then it all mellows out, and I start to enjoy the high. By that time, the sun is an inch above the horizon and even the scrub bushes are casting long shadows. The sunset gives a rosy glow to the desert floor, and it seems like a celebration. Whip-tail lizards chase each other between rocks like little children do when they get wild and silly. A flock of wrens passes overhead with a happy spirit, lifting and chirping. I go with the altered consciousness and let it take me in a cool escape from the day's reality. When night comes, I slip into my bag, enjoy the comforting numbness as it eases into my arms and legs, and I fall into a luxuriously careless sleep.

***

The storm creeps in at dawn. Big booger-size drops splat on my face and raise little dust puffs all around me in the dirt. The sky is dark in water-heavy clouds. A wind gust whips sand in my face when I look out across the desert. I close my eyes and turn away fast. It's a bad mistake, and I'm almost knocked out by the pain of a hundred needles stabbing my brain and a stomach churning dizziness. I recognize the payback for last night's encounter with Jimmy's magic potion.

I squeeze my eyes tight and try to get my head down inside my bag, but the falling water gets so heavy I start to feel a cold wetness coming through my bag—I know I have to get out and get up.

I hear loud voices above the pebble drone of the rain and join everybody in a mad rush for cover. We scramble to pick up packs and sleeping bags. The thunder crashes so hard you can feel the vibration in your stomach like the thump of the big bass drum when it passes in front of you in a parade.

The one tarp we erected last night in the middle of the pine grove is flapping like one of those huge white egret birds on takeoff. We cram in together under it, while Mark and Amy pound in more stakes and lash it down with extra ropes to some of the trees. It's a battle with the power of the rising wind. When they've done their best, they come in all soggy to the center of the tarp with the rest of us.

Everybody gets into their packs for their warmest, driest stuff. We'd all slept in our clothes, but it's cold being wet. We get out our jackets and tarps to wrap up in against the whipped up water.

When the main part of the storm hits, it comes so hard you can't see ten feet away. Thunder mixes with the howl of the wind and the pelting torrent to drown out voices, and we have to shout at each other to be heard. The tarp helps, but it doesn't stop the horizontal gust-blown sprays from wetting us down.

We usually keep a distance from each other, but nature forces us into a close huddle in the middle of our cover. I can't tell you why, but the closeness and common reaction to the storm makes it feel like the counselors are more human and the other kids something like family. It gives me an all-in-this-together sorta feeling.

The storm changes the air, like it's charged with electricity, and there's something fresh about it that makes you feel good.

When lightning flashes in the distance, we all watch. It has the beauty of a fourth of July firework against the dark nothingness. Sometimes it lights the desert like a giant camera flash. I watch it creep toward us, pounding our eardrums with those delayed cracks and booms, until its closeness becomes less beautiful and starts to feel kinda dangerous. We watch a crooked white rope of light touch the top of a tree on a near ridge and the thunder roar is simultaneous with the lightening. My ears pop from the sound pressure, and I feel like I've gone deaf for a minute. The ridge pine bursts into flame like a tiki torch dipped in oil. That's when Mark freaks.

"We can't stay in this pine grove. There's a ravine fifty yards from here, and we're going to have to run for it. Jimmy, I want you to lead the way, down to the lowest spot you can find. I want everybody to follow Jimmy, and I want you to run as fast as you can. Leave your packs. If you can get your tarp out quickly, take it with you. Now go!"

Mark grabs Jimmy by the front of his jacket and pushes him out of the shelter. Jimmy stumbles out into the downpour and starts running. Sam and Katie take up right after him, then Chastity. Mark yells something at me and Kevin, but I can't understand him. Kevin looks stunned, and I grab his arm and he follows me; we run like crazy through rain so thick it's like running through a waterfall. Amy and Mark come last, and they bring their packs. We all get down in the ravine. Mark and Amy pull tarps and survival blankets out of their packs and hand them around. Everybody is soaked to the skin by then.

Mark looks around like he's counting heads.

"Everybody wrap up in whatever you've got. Put your feet together and get your blankets and tarps off the ground. I want you to stoop down and squat on the balls of your feet. Nothing touching the ground but the balls of your feet. Do it. NOW!"

It couldn't be more than a few seconds later that a thunder bolt hits the tallest tree in the pine grove we left minutes before. It turns the trunk into a white-hot pole and the branches into webs of light; the electricity seems to be spraying out into the air all around it. We watch, unable to take our eyes off the light and heat and danger. From the bottom of the trunk, it streaks the ground with veins of blue-white light to the trunks of other trees. Then a flash-fire explodes on the struck tree. It's so hot we can feel it on our faces where we stand. It ignites the surrounding trees, and the whole grove is on fire. I swear I feel an electric charge go through my feet.

"Holy shit," Jimmy says. "That could have been us in that electric roaster."

"Everybody OK?" Mark asks.

Me and Katie and Chastity are hugging each other as we watch our tarp shelter burning and sputtering in the middle of the grove in the rain. The pines burn like candles on a cake, and we feel the heat and smell the burned wood.

"Stay on the balls of your feet, nobody touching anybody else, nothing else touching the ground," Mark says. We break our huddle.

We stay like that for ten minutes. It's hard to balance on your toes, but Mark has earned a lot of cred in the last few minutes so we all obey.

Sam breaks the silence as we crouch there. "Well, it's a good thing we didn't stay over there. Did anybody else feel their feet tingle when our tarp got blasted?"

"I didn't feel anything in my feet, but I could feel my hair kinda standing up on my head," Chastity says.

"Well I don't have all that much hair," Katie says. "But it made my scalp tingle."

"Hey you guys, I think we owe Mark big time for this one," Chastity says.

"Don't be such a brown nose, Chastity," Jimmy D. says.

"Hey, Jimmy, I saw you take off out there like you were being chased by a mad dog," Sam says.

"Yeah, and you looked like you were gonna pass me up—you were runnin' so scared your eyes were popping."

"Oh yeah, well..."

"Enough," Mark says. "Pay attention to what we're doin', we're goin' to be out of here in a little while."

The lightning and thunder pass over us. There's lots more strikes, but they're moving away as the thunder gets less intense.

Amy busies herself trying to cover us from the rain. She doesn't say anything but keeps straightening everybody's cover-ups, tucking them in where they're already tucked. Nothing she does is necessary, and she doesn't have much effect on our comfort. She doesn't look at the grove fire or anything, and finally, Mark takes her by the shoulders.

"Are you OK, Amy?"

At that she breaks down crying like a little kid and grabs him and won't let go. He holds her for awhile. I'm thinking they should be embarrassed, but then all of us kind of understand why Amy freaked after what happened. She calms down and lets him go.

Mark stands up and speaks to all of us. "Hey, you guys did good. If you ever needed a lesson in why you should follow orders, you just got it. If that didn't do it for you, nothing will. Now the rain is letting up, and we are going to have to get going. Everybody lost their packs to the fire except me and Amy, so we're going to have to do the best we can with what we've got."

Kevin had left his sleeping bag and had run to the tarp without his shoes that morning, so we hunt them down and get him some dry socks out of Mark's pack. We go back to the pine grove to recover the remains of our packs. Some of them are burned to a total loss, but one is untouched. Mine had been lying close to the first tree that got hit, so it's nothing but a pile of black steaming muck. I poke around in it until I recover my tin cup and give up on everything else. The sleeping bags that got left out in the rain are drenched and muddy, but we roll and tie them as best we can with the hope of getting them dried out later on.

We're then a bonded team—wet, uncomfortable, and totally exhilarated. That's our attitude when we set out on the trail again for Windy City.

JULIA

When I finish, he says, "Julia! Why didn't you tell me about this when it happened? You could have written me. I would have taken you out of there immediately. I didn't know you were in danger."

I don't answer him right away. I've never told anyone about this before, I don't know why. Maybe it's like when soldiers don't want to talk about being in a war. You know, everybody thinks how daring and brave they were, but they don't want to talk about it because the truth is they were really scared and did stuff they're ashamed of—maybe they weren't brave at all. Or maybe it's that no matter how you tell the story, you know nobody can understand what it was like if they weren't actually there. Telling Dad about the storm experience really brought it back to me, and I don't mind admitting, I was really scared.

We sit in a restaurant booth all the way in the back of the room. We meet right after dance practice, and I feel uncomfortable in public dressed in a bulky sweater over a pink leotard and tights; my hair is still tied up in a tight bun at the back of my head.

"I couldn't, Dad, I told you, they censored our letters. They told us not to whine to our parents about how hard it was. They made us re-write letters they didn't like. I couldn't have told you about it. They wouldn't let me. Didn't you check these people out before you turned me over to them?"

"Of course we did. We weren't happy about sending you there, but it was all we knew to do."

"I don't buy that. You could have talked to me about it first."

"There was no talking to you. That was the problem. We had lost all our influence."

The waitress brings our lunch dishes.

"Is everything OK with you?" she asks with a look of concern that tells me she overheard the last part of our conversation.

"Yes," I say. "We're having some discussion about past history, water under the bridge stuff."

The waitress smiles then, "Enjoy your meal."

We thank her, tear the paper off our chopsticks, and break them apart.

"I think you could have tried harder to work with me," I say. "I was a kid. You had all the cards. You gave up too soon. There were lots of other things you could have done."

"Like what?"

"Lots of things, I don't know, you're the parent."

We sit there in silence for a minute not looking at each other. Finally he looks up as if he's going to say something profound. Instead, he asks, "Julia...I...What happened after that, Julia?"

Here I stand in the silent rain
Wishing for sun to heal my pain
I walk alone and wait by hour
Lonely, lost, bereft of power
Chilling drops be-stripe my face
On cheeks and chin a subtle trace
Tears merge the rain and I succumb
My soul awakes, no longer numb

CHAPTER 21

JULIA

We're back on the trail, and it's still raining, but it's nothing like the downpour we went through with the lightning and all. We walk along in single file with Mark in the lead, splashing through puddles that seem out of place in the desert. The air is fresh, and the scrub-brush looks all perked up and glossy.

I try to think through what happened back there. It's the first time in my life I was actually in deadly danger. It was kind of exciting, like wow, I survived. Did that really happen? Yes, it really did. I'm thinking—here I am, walking in the rain, after almost getting fried by lightning and roasted in a forest fire. The whole scene feels weird to me. Like when you see a really good movie, and your head is so far into the story it's like you're part of it, but then you walk out of the dark theater into the afternoon sunlight. It's kind of a shock to discover it's only another plain old day after all, and you're not sure which is real for a second, the movie or the mall. Am I really hiking in the desert, miles from nowhere, like the rest of the world doesn't exist? Maybe it doesn't. Maybe there are no houses, or stores or roads or cars. Maybe the whole world is like this. Where is my family, my friends? Where's our dog? I feel alone.

My pack is gone. I don't even have the letters to prove I have a family. I'm trying to remember what my dad looks like. How can I not remember what he looks like? Maybe I don't have a mother or a father. Do I really have a sister, or did I make her up too? I don't need to pinch myself because the blisters in my soggy boots prove this is definitely not a dream.

I look up and let the rain fall on my face. With my eyes open, I see the drops plunging down at me. They sting my eyes. A trickle of tears and water stripe my cheeks and neck and run cold into my jacket. I close my eyes and open my mouth to catch the rain drops on my tongue. Is this how it feels to be a refugee, like you see on TV in ragged clothes with swollen bellies? That's how I feel—except for the swollen belly—all I'm doing is trying to survive. No plans, no goals, only living through the next minute so I can have another minute after that. Walking and walking. Why? Why am I doing this? I can't stop, I have to go on. No choice.

I look back to see Kevin behind me. He walks with his head down like he's following my muddy foot prints. His hood covers his face. I wonder what he's thinking. He goes along so accepting, uncaring, like me I guess.

Chastity is ahead of me, a bobbing bundle of tarp and pack. If you didn't know there's a pretty girl in there, you'd think it was a tramp, trudging along in the rain.

We're walking up a low hill with a rain-made river running down. We walk along the side of the water course, but sometimes the water crosses our path so we have to jump it to keep from getting our boots even more soggy. The rivulets combine to form a channel where it washes away the dirt and sand in its path, splashing against big rocks and uncovering small patches of pebbles. That's where I see a glossy black spot in stark contrast against the brown earth. It's at the bottom of the stream under the surface of the muddy water.

I stop to reach for it, but it's gone. Silt washes over it, and it's covered. Then the current brushes the dirt away, and it winks back at me like some dark eye, trying to attract my attention. I'm drawn to its perfect shiny surface. I kneel down and reach into the water for it. It's stuck. The water is cool on my hands, and my knee is getting wet through my pants. I dig around it with my fingers and try to get a better grip on it; the water swirls around my wrists and wets the cuffs of my jacket. It's slippery so I pull with both hands, one wrapped over the other. It still won't move. I step into the stream, a foot on either side of it to get better leverage. I feel my boots filling up with water. It slowly gives to my pull, and I keep the tension on as it inches up out of the ground, slowly exposing its entire length. It's a long skinny obsidian shard that looks like a black knife-blade, all wet and shiny and sharp.

I'm holding it in front of me, turning it over, when Kevin comes, head down, and bumps into my elbow. My hand slips up the blade and slices my finger. It's a deep clean cut, and a pain spike shoots through my hand and up my arm like an electric shock. I shake it off and put pressure on the gash with my thumb to stop the red dripping into the water.

"Hey, that looks like a weapon," he says. "Did it cut you?" I can tell he wants me to give it to him.

"I'm OK. Don't say anything. I'm going to keep it," I say and tuck it in under my tarp. We move on.

"How much farther, Julia? I'm getting tired," he says to the back of my head.

"I have no idea, could be an hour, maybe more."

"My feet hurt."

"Hey Kevin, does it feel kinda weird out here right now, like we're in some strange world or something?"

"No, it don't matter. Nothin' ever changes."

"Do you remember what your dad looks like?" I ask.

"Yeah, he's tall and always wears a suit and tie."

"No, I mean his face. Can you see his face?"

"Yeah, kinda. I don't remember what he looks like if I'm like looking at him, but I remember a picture of him. I can see the picture in the frame, and I can remember what he looks like from that," Kevin says

"I wish I could remember what my dad looks like."

"Maybe you can get him to send you a picture."

***

We finally make it to the Windy City camp, and it's getting dark. The rain stops, the sky clears, and the first stars appear. The van with the food drop is there waiting for us. We're all exhausted; still, we get up a shelter so we can have a fire, and each make our tarp tents. We get a hot fire going and take off pieces of clothing one at a time, holding them to the fire on the end of a stick. We all have blisters from walking in wet boots and socks. A box of bandages goes around while we dry our clothes. I get my socks dry, and it feels wonderful to put the warm socks on over my bandaged feet.

I look at the red lit faces around the fire and think about who these kids are. We shared a real danger and survived it together. That bond and the warm fire are comforting, and everyone is in a good mood. Amy and Mark are preparing to leave with the van driver. They huddle with their replacements, Jordan and Travis. Left alone around the fire, all the kids get talking. Even tight-lipped Katie opens up.

"This reminds me of some rainy days in Portland—which seemed like most of the time—when I was following a grunge band around the northwest," she says.

"I saw one of those bands in Seattle a year ago; I tried to get them to let me rap with them" Jimmy D. says.

"I had a thing going with the lead guitar player," Katie says. "I wet my pants when he played the high notes; it was like the screaming vibrations were candy for my brain. I felt like I was up there on the stage with him. He looked so into it and happy, and I felt the same with the music. He looked down at me and the feeling stayed with me, and it was there even when we made love at night after the concert. Then they went to Chicago, and I couldn't get there for the show. I never saw him again, but we had fun when they were touring around here."

Chastity says, "Like you were a groupie?"

"Oh yeah! There were four of us. Sometimes the band would let us come up on the stage and hula-hoop while they played. We lived in a VW bus, and we made money for food, gas, and concert tickets by selling hot cheese sandwiches in the parking lot at the shows. That's why I'm here. My parents couldn't handle it when they didn't hear from me for three months. It sure was fun while it lasted."

"You gotta be kiddin', cheese sandwiches?" Sam says.

"Yeah, we had a generator, and we'd set up an ironing board next to the van to make sandwiches with a steam iron. All you need is a brick of yellow cheese, a pound of butter, and a loaf of white bread. It didn't really toast the bread, but the cheese melted. We could sell 'em as fast as we could make 'em. Everybody had the munchies at those concerts. We got two bucks a piece for 'em, and we were set by the time the concert started. If we needed gas money, we'd sell more after the concert when the parking lot was jammed and all those stoned kids were hanging out waiting for the traffic to die down. One of the guys on the bus had a connection and sold a little weed too."

Kevin brightened up, "I wish I had one of those cheese sandwiches right now."

"I'd buy one," Jimmy D. says.

"Yeah, I got pretty sick of cheese sandwiches, but I could go for one right now too," Katie says.

We're all feeling pretty relaxed when the new counselor Travis comes over. As soon as Amy and Mark are gone with the van, he's starts in on us.

"What are you talking about? We're not going to sit around gossiping and drying out our clothes one piece at a time. Which one are you?" he says pointing at Jimmy D.

Jimmy takes his time to answer. I can tell this is not going to be a good start. "Jimmy," he finally says. He gets up in slow motion, looks at me like he wants me to join a rebellion, but I don't move. He sticks his hands in his pockets and stands with his feet wide apart and his head cocked to one side.

"I want you to get some sticks and make up a drying rack. You help him," he says pointing at Sam. "Make it big enough to hold everybody's stuff. The rest of you change out of your wet clothes and put on some dry things. Pile your wet stuff over here."

Nobody moves. Sam looks at Jimmy who stands there with two clenched fists and a jaw so tight I can see the muscles in his face swell; then they both look at me. I slowly shake my head.

Travis turns to Jimmy. "What are you waiting for?"

I jump up and step between the two of them.

"We don't have any dry stuff, everything got wet," I tell Travis.

"That's totally irresponsible. We'll have no more of that. Take off your wet clothes and wrap up in the blankets that came with the food drop until your clothes are dry," Travis says.

I give Jimmy a push as he and Sam start moving away.

That's when Jordan comes over. She takes Travis aside. We can hear his side of the conversation. "I don't care," he keeps saying and "So what, it doesn't matter." He throws up his hands in a gesture to Jordan, spins around and comes right back at us.

"You and you," he says pointing at me and Chastity, "get the supplies the van dropped and bring them over here. I don't want anybody getting into those supplies without my permission. You'll bring them all over here, and I'll issue out to those who can show me they need it."

"Why are you two sitting there?" Now it's Katie and Kevin's turn. "Get up and help them get the supplies over here," Travis says.

Katie jumps up and comes with me and Chastity. Kevin doesn't move. He holds his sock-on-a-stick out to the fire and doesn't even look up.

Travis comes over and stands next to him and yells. "Didn't you hear me, get up and help with those supplies."

Kevin ignores him. Everybody stops to watch.

"I said get up." Travis grabs a handful of the back of Kevin's jacket and pulls him up standing. Jimmy D. starts to move toward Travis, but Sam blocks him with his arm. The sock Kevin holds out on his stick falls off and catches fire. Kevin stands there, watching it burn.

"I said go help with the supplies," Travis yells again as his face turns red and ugly.

Kevin doesn't move. Travis spins him around so they're face-to-face. Jordan hurries over and steps in between Kevin and Travis.

"I'll handle this, Travis," she says in a tone that surprises everybody, and Travis takes a step back.

"We can't let him get away with this," he says.

"I've got it. You take care of the others," she says, her eyes locked on his. They stare at each other for a moment, then Travis drops his head, turns toward us and juts out his jaw.

"Stop gawking, all of you. I want all those supplies here in five minutes. Get that drying rack set up right now. Those other counselors might let you get away with it, but that's over—and he's not getting away with this either, you'll see," he says pointing back at Kevin. We all turn back to our assignments.

Jordan takes Kevin aside, gives him a sock for his bare foot out of her pack, and tells him to stay put.

Travis isn't a big guy; in fact, he's short and his head's so big it looks out of proportion, kinda like a midget or a bobble-head doll. That's it, like a bobble-head, you know, with a big wobbly head and arms and legs that are too short for the body. He isn't a midget though; he only kinda gives that impression a little bit when you first look at him. His hair is cut so short he's almost bald. Everybody always says short guys have a complex like that French guy Napoleon, but I think Travis really does. He'd probably make us salute him if Jordan would let him get away with it.

And Travis knows everything about everything. When we build a shelter, it has to be just so. If we're making a fire, it's either too big or too small. He claims he can tell the weather by looking at the clouds and feeling the wind. He's about as good at it as the TV weatherman, which isn't very good. Oh yeah, Travis is in charge, and he wants everybody to know it.

Jordan, on the other hand, is easy going and real. You feel like she's on our side. We aren't only a chore to her. She's tall for a girl; it kinda makes the two of them look like Mutt and Jeff. And she's pretty. I mean, there's a classic beauty about her, none of that "beauty is in the eye of the beholder stuff"—there isn't anybody that wouldn't agree that she is beautiful. She lets

Travis boss her around too, but only on the small stuff. If it's important, like when Travis gets us lost, she steps up and keeps things on track.

We hike for four days in a row after that big storm. They have names for all the camps. Two miles to Kanobi, three to Bear, five miles in one day to Panda. When we get to Tweedy, there's a food drop and some mail. We set up camp for a couple of days.

I get five letters all at one time, four from my dad full of the same old bullshit, and one from Bree that cheers me up.

Kevin gets one letter.

"You want to read my letter, Julia?" he says. "It's from my mom."

He won't leave me alone 'til I read it. It's typed on really thin pink paper, and it smells like cinnamon.

> Dear Kevin,
>
> We were happy to get your letter and glad to hear that you are doing fine. Your father and I are leaving this week for Europe, and we'll be gone for a month or two. If you need anything, you can contact your Aunt Silvia through the wilderness people. I'm sure you won't be completing your program before we get back.
>
> I hope you have been thinking about what you've done and are ready to apply yourself when you return to school. Your father's attorney is arranging a new boarding school for you when you are ready. In the meantime, do what they tell you and don't cause any more trouble. Don't write us any more letters because we won't get them until we get back.
>
> Love, Mother.

"Well that's good Kevin; she wrote back right away," I say. I'm thinking that was the meanest letter I'd ever seen, but I don't want to make Kevin feel bad.

"Yeah, I guess I won't need to write any more letters for a while."

"Hey, you can read my letters, my dad's a writing fool. He's got enough advice for both of us." We laugh. I wish I could do something for Kevin, but I don't know how. Here he is, stinkin' rich and his life is miserable because nobody gives a damn about him.

Wow! This is my life
Reality cuts like a dull metal knife
This may cause strong distress
I close my eyes and take a breath.

CHAPTER 22

JULIA

T hen Travis comes up with another stupid idea. I swear he lays awake at night dreaming up ways to screw things up. Solo. I trudge along with my gear on my back in the direction they point. "Walk until you can't see us anymore and set up camp," Travis says. "You'll be there by yourself for at least twenty-four hours. We'll let you know when it's time to come back. You're on your own until then."

I'm relieved, really. Nobody looking over my shoulder. Nobody telling me what to do every minute. I wish I could tell where we are. If I knew what direction to go, I'd keep right on walking out of here. I could stretch out the food and water for three or four days. If they aren't lying and I have a full day's head start, I might be able to find a rancher to help me. All those cow patties don't plop out of wild cows, that's for sure. There's got to be a cowboy around here somewhere.

I walk a crooked path, weaving around the sagebrush and bunch grasses. Every once in a while I scare up a lizard. There's one that runs in front of me. He isn't smart enough to slither off to the side. He gets a few feet ahead of me and stops. When I come up on him again, he fast-crawls away. It's kinda like kicking a can. I zone on watching him until he finally gets wise, takes off out of my path, and disappears under a bush. I feel lonely without him.

I head straight for a single juniper tree which is the only feature breaking the straight line of the horizon. When I look back toward camp, I can't see them anymore. I think about being all alone and running back, but then it passes—and I keep on for the tree.

My shelter needs something to hold it up. The juniper is all there is, so I wrap a rope on it as high up as I can reach, tie the other end around a big rock, and stretch the rope tight so I can throw my tarp over it. I don't have any stakes, but I stretch the sides out and hold the edges down with more rocks. It's kinda lop-sided. Travis would make me do it over, but it's good enough for me. It will keep the dew off me and my stuff.

I get hungry, and I realize I can totally eat whatever I want, whenever I want. I rummage around in my food packs to see what looks best. The first thing I eat is the orange Jimmy D. tried to get away from me to make his crazy hooch. I'm never going for that again. The orange is sweet and makes me even hungrier. The only other thing I have that doesn't need heating up is some biscuits, so I eat those until I feel satisfied.

I sit down on the sand in front of the tent, lean back against my pack, pull off my boots, and stretch my sore legs straight out in front of me. That's all I plan to do. It's quiet. I close my eyes. I hear the hum of a bug circle my head twice like it's looking for a good landing spot. Without opening my eyes, I wave my hand around my head. When it finally buzzes off, I let my body completely relax. I'm tired.

It's almost dark when I wake up. I see the first stars, and know it's going to be a cloudless night. In the desert, that means it's going to be cold. I get on my sweater and my jacket and start looking around for some firewood. There isn't much, but I only need enough to heat up some water. I find some small sticks and a dry cow patty. No matches, of course. We're too dangerous for matches. I get out my bow drill kit and trim up the spindle with the obsidian blade. It takes me a while to start a fire, but I finally get it going and cook up some ten grain.

When I finish eating, it's pitch black. No moon, only a zillion stars. I have a feeling somebody's watching me. People are always saying they have a feeling somebody's watching them. I know it's stupid to think that, but I look around anyway without seeing anything. There isn't much to do but go to sleep. I roll out my bag in the shelter and bring in my pack and all the other stuff, including my bow drill kit and the obsidian blade so they won't be wet in the morning. I leave the unwashed cup and wood spoon by the dying fire.

Every night I fall asleep thinking about home. I think about my warm bed or sitting in front of the wood stove with a red-hot fire going and Mom's terrier in my lap. I miss my sister and my mom and dad. I wonder if they're even thinking about me. I think about everything I've been through in the last year. That stuff's so far away now, like it happened to somebody else.

I start to drift off, but the clang of my cup on a rock brings me out of it. It sounds like something is pushing the cup across the sand. I think it must be a ground squirrel or a rabbit snacking on the crumbs I left in the tin. It stops after a minute. I snuggle a little deeper into my bag and close my eyes.

I haven't gotten to sleep yet when a rustling of my tent tarp rouses me again. It could be the wind blowing the tent, but it sounds more like something scratching the tarp. I hear an animal sniffing. It's on the side of the tent where my pack is. Animals have good noses for food. Mom's terrier can sniff out a dog biscuit in a jacket pocket, and I figure a squirrel could do it too. I hit the side of the tent to scare it away, and it stops.

The moon has come up. I see silver light on the juniper needles outside the open end of the tent. I lay with my head at the small end, my feet at the opening. An animal crosses in front of the tent opening, then another and another. They aren't squirrels or rabbits, that's for sure.

The shadowy profiles look like scrawny dogs about the size of small shepherds, their heads hanging low. Coyotes. I heard them last night at the camp. Travis says they're shy of humans, and they'd never let us see them. Right again, Travis.

I can hear them outside, pacing around the tent, poking at the cup again. Then one gives out that weird yipping bark they do. The others join in, and they take turns like their building each other up. The creepy howling raises the hair on the back of my neck. I sit up and pull my arms out of my sleeping bag. One of them looks into the tent, then darts off. When he comes back, I throw one of my boots at him. It misses, but it scares him. He jumps back and goes away. The animal noises get louder. I worry I've made him mad. I'm not so far away from the camp they won't be able to hear them. I'm sure Travis will be on his way to scare them off. I pull my knees up to my chest and get as far back in the tent as I can. I pull my pack around in front of me.

When they go quiet again, I listen in the silent night to try and figure out where they are. I'm totally blind except for what I can see at the triangle opening. I hold my breath to listen for the smallest sounds. I know they're circling because I see their shadows in silhouette when they pass between the tent and the moon, again and again. The biggest one comes around to the opening, and I can see him plainly. The moonlight shines off the silver fur of his pointy ears and the wet tip of his brown nose. He stands there looking at me for seconds that seem like hours. Our eyes lock; he has clear mean eyes. I can't stop shaking and try to back up as far as I can in the tent. I'm afraid he senses my fear. He lunges at my pack and darts back, then lunges again and takes hold of a piece of the pack in his jaws. I hold onto the shoulder straps and yell at him.

"Git, go, go away, hey, hey, hey."

His jaws are clamped tight on my pack, tugging hard. I pull back. When he tears a piece loose, I fall back against the tent and worry I might knock it down on myself. A second coyote joins the first, and they stare at me at the entrance.

"Go, git, go away."

They howl at me together with open mouths and the moonlight sparkles off the tips of their teeth. I grope around me in the dark for my other boot and feel a sharp burn when my hand brushes the razor edge of the obsidian blade. Warm blood wets my hand, and the coyotes start sniffing at the air. The howls grow louder, and they get bolder as the two of them creep further into the tent. The big one jumps on my pack with his front paws and lunges at my face. I take a hard grip on that obsidian and slash it across his snout. He draws back, and I find my other boot with my free hand. When he lunges again, I hit him hard on the nose with the boot in one hand and swing the black blade at him with the other, but I miss. I can see blood dripping from his nose where the obsidian connected the first time. Then there are three of them in the entrance, and their howling and yipping whips up. The leader makes another lunge, and I put my arm up to shield my face. He grabs my arm in his jaws right above the wrist. I can feel the points of his teeth through my denim jacket. With my right hand, I ram the sharp tip of the obsidian straight at him. I miss his snout, but I pull his head up with the arm he holds in his jaws and aim for the side of his neck. The blade digs deep right under his chin. When I pull the obsidian out, I feel a wet stream squirting out pulses like a tiny lawn sprinkler. He stumbles back, pulling me by the arm on top of my pack, then lets go when his front legs collapse as he tries to back out of the mouth of the tent. The others run as the leader falls on his side. He lays there panting, oozing blood in a puddle around his head and shoulders. He isn't dead. His eyes are on me, unblinking, and his jaws open and close as if trying hard to get a breath. I don't know where the others are. My wrist aches from the jaw grip, and my hand bleeds from the obsidian cut, but I hold onto that blade and sit there watching the animal die. We stare at each other until his panting finally stops as his eyes slowly glaze over like a window fogging on a cold night. I know he's gone. Still, I can't move.

It's quiet, but for the sound of my sobs. I don't know how long I sit there staring at that dead coyote, but I don't stir until the glow of the rising sun begins warming me through the tent tarp. I cut open the small end of the tent and crawl out into the morning sunshine. I'm still holding the obsidian blade. I look at my hand. The blood has dried, but there's a lot of it. I look around for signs of the other animals. Their footprints in the dirt and my tumbled tin cup are the only signs. My wooden spoon is gone.

I sit facing the rising sun, holding the obsidian blade in front of me in my uninjured hand. I cry. I cry for myself, for my fear, for my loneliness. I cry for what I've done, for my dad's protection, for my mother's arms. I cry for them and home.

The sun is at my back when Travis finds me sitting there.

"What's going on Julia?"

I can't answer him. He looks around and sees the dead coyote. He shakes me and asked me again. When I don't answer or look at him, he says he'll be right back and takes off running.

Jordan comes. She sits down next to me and doesn't say anything. She opens my fingers one by one and takes the obsidian blade from my hand. Then she wraps her arms around me and holds me for a long time. I let her. I stop crying.

"I'm OK," I say.

"Let me see your hand. We're going to clean you up."

She has a first aid kit and washes my hand, putting antiseptic on it. The sting of the medicine brings me around.

"I'm OK," I say again.

"Looks like you had quite a night, Julia. You want to talk about it?"

"No."

She wraps my hand in some bandages and tapes it up.

"You hurt anywhere else?"

"You might look at my other wrist."

She pushes back my jacket and sweater sleeves. My arm has a blue bruise, but there are no cuts or anything. She asks me to move my hand and wrist. It's sore, but nothing broken.

"What happened Julia? What happened last night?"

I stand up and look around my camp. Everything is peaceful under the setting sun. I go over to the mouth of the tent and look down at the coyote, lying in a stain of brown blood.

"This is what happened," I say. "This is what fucking happened!"

Something powerful snaps in me, and I start kicking the animal with my bare feet. I hear myself screaming at the dead animal. I kick until my bare toes are hurting. She tries to pull me back, but I lose my balance and fall on it. I start beating it with my fists. When she finally pulls me off, I struggle to kick it some more. She manages to stand me back up and holds me tight against her, and I stop struggling. She pulls me away from the camp and the coyote and turns me around and looks at me.

"Julia, I'm sorry."

"Sorry?" I'm crying again. "You guys left me out here in the middle of the goddamn wilderness with no protection in the middle of the goddamn night and *this*"—I point at the coyote—"*This* is what happened." I'm having trouble catching my breath. "How could you do this to me? Didn't you hear them howling?"

She tries to grab me again, but I back away. "You are supposed to be helping me, not feeding me to the goddamn animals. Do you have any idea what it's like to be out here all alone with no protection and be attacked by a pack of wild dogs? I could have been killed. I want out of here. I want you to call whoever you need to call and tell them to come and get me and take me back home. I want out of here now, and you better do it."

"Now Julia, it's going to be all right, let's..."

"No, it is not going to be all right. I want out of here now."

"We'll work this out, Julia; let's get you back to camp for now."

Jordan gets me some fresh socks from her pack. She finds my boots and helps me get them on because of my wrapped hand.

"Let's you and I go back to camp now. We'll have Travis and a couple of the boys come back here for your stuff."

I pick up the obsidian blade.

"Better leave that with the other stuff," she says.

"Oh no, this is going with me wherever I go until I get back home. Don't even think of taking this from me."

"OK," she says. "OK, let's go."

***

Everybody wants to know what happened, but Travis and Jordan won't let me talk about it. Sam and Jimmy D. know because they went with Travis to bury the coyote and pick up my camp. Jimmy D. tells me he's gonna write a rap about it, and Sam says the coyote must have been rabid to attack a human like that. Katie and Chastity help me do stuff I can't do because of the bandaged hand. They all want to see the dagger I used to kill the coyote, but I won't show it. Kevin saw it when I found it, and he makes a big deal about telling everybody what it looks like and how sharp it is.

INTERLUDE

STEVEN

The thought of Julia fighting a wild animal was so incongruous I had trouble picturing it. "You killed a coyote?" I said, cringing at the realization I was responsible for causing my daughter to face a mortal danger all alone.

"Hey, he was about to chew on me, Dad."

"He probably only wanted your food, you know."

"Oh yeah, I should have asked him if he would like some chicken feed instead of the chicken. Right. Yes, I killed the damn coyote. I was scared to death." She wasn't bragging. She got up from the table and paced the room. I could tell it was a vivid memory for her. When she sat back down, she gave me a look that said "don't challenge me on this." I changed the subject.

"Is that what the piece of black glass in the box is? Is that the blade you stabbed him with?"

"I wouldn't let them have it. I told them if they tried to take it away from me I was going to start screaming and not stop until I passed out or they took me home. At first Travis tried to bully me into giving it up, but he gave up pretty quick when I started screaming. Jordan tried to reason with me, but that didn't work for her either. I think they were worried about getting into trouble over the whole thing and especially because my hand was cut up pretty good. I kept that blade the rest of my time out there. I didn't show it around, but I always knew exactly where it was in case I needed it."

"I'm sorry Julia. If we'd known anything like that was going to happen to you, we never would have sent you there. You know that don't you?"

"Yes, I know that. What was mom doin' while I was fighting-off the savage beasts?"

CHAPTER 23

MARY

S teven worked on me until I finally agreed to help him with Julia's room. It was hard to go in there. It felt like a crime scene. There was no blood to clean up, but there were plenty of ugly reminders of what was going on in my daughter's life. It made me want to cry for my baby, and it made me mad at the kids who'd used her.

It all had to go. The graffiti looked like a south LA street scene. The most common word was "fuck." It was hard to imagine this was my child. There was nothing very original except for a limerick scrawled on the back of the door.

> There's a blonde headed boy in my class
> With a beautifully cute little ass,
> If he wasn't so shy
> Each day I pass by,
> I'd give him a roll in the grass.

I brushed two coats of stain blocker on the poem and three coats on a piece of graffiti penned-in below it, "Julia is a whore." It was signed in cursive by "Ima Slut." This was part of my daughter's life, the sweet baby I once fed from my breasts and rocked to sleep in my arms; the little girl who once loved me so much, but now told me she hated me. It made my stomach tight, and I wanted to run from the room. Only Steven's optimism kept me there.

The sliding mirror doors on the closet had a list of boys' names written in lipstick, some with check marks after them as if they were chores done or a record of progress toward a goal of some kind. Steven scrubbed them off without comment, but the intensity in his whirling rag made his feelings about them quite clear. I scraped off the marijuana leaves she'd glued to the wall to finish the canopy over a sketched-in tree trunk. The window was covered in rock band logos, along with one social commentary sticker which I actually approved of. They always tell you to start with shared ground and work from there. Like that would work with Julia.

I kept trying to figure out where I'd lost her. She was never an easy child, but she was always loving. We butted heads a lot before, but something changed between us. It was almost a character change. She seemed to have lost all intimate connection to us. Like what happens when people fall in love, but I know that wasn't it. She wasn't mooning over some boy. It was more like she was angry about everything. You couldn't speak to her about anything without making her mad. I think she knew she was doing wrong and had a shame about it that wouldn't let her admit it to herself or to us.

Steven brought in a step ladder and pulled the glow-in-the-dark stars and planets off the ceiling.

"You think she's safe?" he asked. "There could be poisonous snakes or wild animals out there."

"Don't be ridiculous. You're such a worrier. Those people know what they're doing. They struck me as professionals, and I feel they care about Julia. They like her. I can tell by the phone reports. I'm sure she's fine. They'd tell us if there were any problems, wouldn't they?"

"Yeah, I'm sure they would. Travis and Jordan seemed a little subdued on that last conference call, but maybe they were over-tired from being out in the field for so long. I hope we get this done before it's time for her to come home," Steven said.

He levered the lid off a five-gallon bucket of lavender paint with a screw driver and started mixing it with the flat stick the store gave him.

"It's OK by me if she stays with them for a while," I said. "I'm not ready for her to come home. At least I know she's safe, and I don't have to put up with her tantrums. It's been a relief to sleep through the night and not have to wonder where she is or what she's doing."

"Do you think we did the right thing, Mary, handing her over to a bunch of strangers? Maybe we could have kept her here and worked it out."

"Oh my god, Steven, are you still questioning yourself? Oh no, there wasn't any other way. I would have gone insane if we hadn't done something. We did the right thing, I'm sure of it, and don't you go second guessing yourself."

I held out the roller pan while Steven poured paint from the bucket.

"Well, I still feel guilty. I could have gotten more involved like you said. I should have done something when we first recognized things were going wrong, but I expected her to figure things out and get back on track without our help. She's always been so smart. I didn't think she'd lose control."

"But you did try," I said. "You wrote that contract, and she agreed to it. She promised to attend all of her classes and do all of her homework, and you offered to help her with it. She agreed to it, then immediately ignored it."

"Yeah, she agreed to it, but she wouldn't sign it. I should have made her sign it."

"Stop it!" I said. "You are not guilty. You did everything you could; she wouldn't come half-way."

"I know you're right, but I still feel like I let her down."

Steven had the ceiling job. When he climbed up on the ladder, I looked up at him. This was classic Steven; he always saw things from the other person's perspective. He gave the other person the benefit of the doubt whether they deserved it or not. He took all the responsibility when things went wrong. It made him an easy target for the less scrupulous among us. Some would call him compassionate. I think he's plain old naïve sometimes. On the other hand, I've seen what happens when he discovers somebody being purposefully underhanded or deceiving—you do not ever want to be on that side of Steven.

"Don't even think of calling it off," I said. "There is no way I'm ready for her to come home. We have to trust those people to help her and send her back with a better attitude when the time is right and not before. She'll be fine. We have to stay with this. The longer she's gone, the better."

"It's just that it's hard for me now, not to be able to do anything but write letters. I hate the thought that she might feel abandoned." I could see the sadness in the eyes looking down at me from the step ladder. "You know how she's always been afraid to be alone," Steven said.

"She's not alone; she's with a bunch of other kids and under the eye of those counselors all the time. She's probably having the other problem— no privacy."

"Are those kids still calling to find out what happened to her?"

"Only Maggie," I said. "The rest of them don't seem to care anymore. Bree had a little run-in with Darla, but that's about it. They've had their little drama over it, but they've worn it out and moved on since Julia isn't here to participate."

"Well those kids are history. She's not going to have anything to do with them when she comes back, I guarantee you that."

"What are we going to do? She has to go back to school," I said.

"Not that school. There's nothing wrong with the school, but she is not going back to that crowd. We're going to put her in a different high school, miles away. It'll be a bus ride. I have a friend in that district. We can use their address."

Steven climbed back down and put his arm around my waist; we looked at our handy work.

"Hey, it's starting to look pretty good in here with the graffiti covered up," Steven said. "Let's pick this up tomorrow. I'm going to write Julia a letter before we go to bed."

Here I stand a shadow
Of my life
Without control I watch
It dance by
I see my problems
I see myself cry
Here I am
And here I lie
Patient thoughts
A deep slow breath
Time
Will have to heal the rest.

CHAPTER 24

JULIA

The hike from Windy City to Bear is a full day. It's already hot when we leave in the morning, so I know it's going to be a cooker. They say it's ten miles. I don't know, but we hike all day—nothing ever changes. If I had to give my opinion on the nature of the world right now, I would say it is flat as a pancake and dry as bone. There is no trail, so we're at the mercy of Travis's sense of direction, which I have my doubts about, but I play along with follow-the-leader. I suspect we're taking a few wrong turns because we don't seem to be going toward the same distant hills, but I don't know for sure. I feel a little better when Jordan pulls out her compass, and we make a sharp left toward the low sun.

We trudge along in single file, the line stretching out as the day wears on. Travis and Jordan walk up and down the line checking on us every so often. Nobody speaks much; it's too hot to talk and easier to walk if you kind of lean forward and keep your head down to balance the weight of the pack.

I haven't thought so hard or so deep in a long time. I feel like I'm going deep, below the obtuse problems or surface ones, like not listening or my anger. I think about the things that cause those. I'm fifteen and to tell the truth, in some ways, I feel like fifty. It's like, for my age, I've been through so much and always have these deep thoughts about stuff that I never bring out or rarely discuss. I never feel able to completely explain myself to anyone. I know I have so much more to experience, but it's hard to imagine that because I feel I've experienced so much already. It sounds odd, but it makes sense in my head. So many things are like that in my journal at home. I wrote to get my feelings out, but it ended up being these long pages of endless chatter and nonsense. I could never get out all I felt because on paper it never made sense. It's like the things I think cannot be put into words, but they do exist. Putting all that away, I'm beginning to find myself. Maybe it's my new self. I don't know, but I like it.

Everything is settling into place, but being away from everybody makes me feel like something is missing. I think I might get a chance to talk to David tomorrow. He really is a good person to talk to. I smile at the picture of Michelangelo's statue popping into my mind. He makes me feel a lot better when I talk to him. He does seem to understand me. I have so many thoughts running through my head all the time, and it gets so old after awhile. I keep dreaming of home and waking up to not being there. It makes me not want to dream at all. I think about all the things in my head and wonder what to do with them. Lately I have sorted them out, thought about them, dealt with them as much as possible, and tucked some of them away.

It's weird, but I don't think about my friends that much. When I was with them, I considered them more important than my family most of the time. I guess what they say is true, family is more important. I have lots of time to think about so much and look inside myself. I still see what was always there, except I realize I needed to pull it out to stop living in a dream world and stop telling myself things are okay that aren't—or that my parents are always wrong.

The straps on my pack are making my shoulders ache, and the pain brings me out of my zone. We are all getting tired toward the end, and the counselors are getting less strict about us talking to each other. That's how I get a chance to talk to Katie. I'm walking along way behind Jimmy D., and I'm alone with my thoughts when we enter a wooded grove in the late afternoon. I stop to re-tie my boot, and Katie catches up with me.

"Hey, Julia, do you think they know where they're taking us?"

I lean my pack way back against a tree and enjoy the relief from the load; then I pull my knee up so I can reach my boot without bending down to tie the laces.

"Hi, Katie. Is this the longest hike or what?"

"It's going on forever," she says. "We're kinda getting strung out now. There's not even a counselor in sight."

"Yeah, wanna make a run for it?"

Katie's eyes widened.

"Hey, I'm kidding." I start back on the trail with Katie following close behind me.

"It has been done you know," she says.

"Yeah, like that could happen with the eagle eyes on us every minute and no where to run."

"Oh no, there were two guys in this program that did it. Kevin told me about it. It was when he first got here."

"Really? They must have freaked when that happened," I say over my shoulder.

"You have no idea. These two guys did it in the middle of the night. You know how they always take our shoes at night and put them in the lock-up bag? They do that because of those guys."

"How did they do it?"

"It was after a long hike like this one, when the counselors were real tired. Kevin said he couldn't sleep for all the loud snoring going on in the shelter, and he saw them. One guy woke up the other guy. They saw Kevin was awake and signaled him to be quiet, and they snuck out of the shelter and hit the road. Well, not the road, but you know what I mean. They'd figured out where the camp was and headed south for the highway. They took their packs, and Kevin saw them get in the counselor's backpack and take a hick saw."

"Kevin saw this?"

"He told me, but he never said anything to the counselors."

"Did they get away with it?"

"What happened was, they stumbled onto a ranch house a couple of miles from the camp, and they held up the rancher in the middle of the night."

"You're kidding!"

"They woke him up and threatened him with the hick saw. They cut his phone line, took his cell phone, and stole his pick-up. The rancher tried to follow them on his tractor. He didn't have any other way." Katie and I laughed at the thought of the farmer bouncing along at top speed on his orange tractor in hot pursuit of the boys in the pickup.

"When the counselors woke up and found them gone, they really panicked. They called in to their office, and the search was on. The rancher got to a phone about the same time, and the cops picked them up on Highway 395. They were probably headed for Reno."

"Who were the counselors?"

"I don't know, but Kevin said they got fired."

"What happened to the two guys?"

"They were arrested for assault and stealing a truck. That's all Kevin knew. He never saw them again. It was all in the papers, and when Kevin's parents found out about it, they sent their lawyers here, who insisted on seeing him. That's how he knew about the rancher and all. Then their lawyers threatened the company with legal action if anything happened to Kevin. That's why he gets away with everything. They're scared to death of him."

"Well, if I was going to run for it, I wouldn't be that stupid."

"Oh yeah, what would you do?"

"First of all, I'd head west, where the sun sets. I have no idea where we are, but I know that if you head west, you're going to hit a river or the Pacific Ocean sooner or later, and there are towns that way."

"What else?" Katie asks.

"I'd do it when they set me up for a solo. That way, I'd at least have a head start on them."

"Right, you could kill a few coyotes for food and live off the land."

"OK, smart ass. I guess I deserved that."

Jordan comes walking back toward us from the head of the line of hikers. "What are you two talking about? Let's separate a little. No talking. We're almost there." She stops Katie while I walk on.

I look back at Katie. We can't help smiling at each other over our little fantasy.

I spend the rest of the hike thinking about what I would do if I made an escape. I think about who I would call for help if I got to a phone. I know Mike would be happy to hear from me, but I'm not sure if he could actually do anything that would help me. Bree would try to help me, but she would be more worried about me and probably tell me to go back and turn myself in. I don't want to owe Darla any favors, that's for sure. When I get down to it, there's really only one person in the whole world I know I could count on, who would know what to do, drop everything the minute I called and come running. That would be my dad.

The heat-waves from the fire blur
And smear reality.
Everything is truly there
But it isn't what should be.

CHAPTER 25

JULIA

I want to wash my hair more than anything. I have no idea what I look like, but it feels gritty and stringy. It reaches my shoulders. They offered to cut it off, but I won't let them. Most of the time, I wear it in two fat braids. I imagine I look like an Indian squaw, but it stays out of my face. There isn't anybody here I care about impressing with flowing curls, so to speak.

Travis takes the boys out on a day hike so we girls can have a little privacy while we wash. Jordan gets a hot fire going and warms up water in the Dutch oven, a big cast iron pot we use for cooking group meals. Chastity and I make a washing stall out of some tarps and rough poles so nobody will see us if they come back.

"I'm goin' first," I say. "I've been waiting too long for this."

Nobody argues. Chastity helps me roll back my collar so I can bend forward and let the water run down over my head and hair without getting my clothes wet. It doesn't really work out that well because the hot water surprises me. I straighten up and bang my head on the pot. The water goes down my back anyway, and I get the shivers.

"Hey, that was hot. You tryin' to scald me?"

"Sorry Julia, it didn't feel so hot on my hand. Guess your neck and scalp are a little more sensitive," Jordan says.

They dry me off, then come at me with another pot of water. After three rinses, I decide it's as good as it gets. Chastity and Katie take their turns while we pour the water over each of them. Katie's wash is more of a scalp scrub after the buzz job that removed the Mohawk, but there's a little fuzz starting to grow. She doesn't look so silly as before. Jordan takes a turn too. We all know she'll get a real shower soon, but it makes us feel like she's a good sport. I really think she understands us pretty good.

"Well, with all the testosterone gone for awhile, you ladies want to have a little hen party?" Jordan asks.

"Yeah, let's get around the fire and dry our hair while we talk," Chastity says.

Jordan gets a brush out of her pack, and we trade-off brushing each other's hair. I almost feel normal for a change. We put the pot of water back on to make some tea and settle in around the fire.

"I'll be so glad to get back to civilization after this," Chastity says. "I'm going to take showers twice a day and spend the rest of the day in a spa, paint my nails, and get totally dressed up every night to go dancing with all the boys one by one."

"Dancing, yeah, I miss that, but not with boys. I mean not to popular music like in a dance party. I like ballet," I tell them.

"Julia, we didn't know. How long have you been dancing?" Jordan asks.

"Since I was five years old—I think—since I was real little anyway. My mom always had me and my sister in a dance school. I kinda lost it in the last year or so. I really miss dancing."

"So you like, wear a tutu and those satin shoes?" Katie says.

"Yeah, for performances. They're called point shoes, and they make your legs look like they're a mile long. It's hard at first, but point shoes are the goal of every ballet student from the beginning. You have to work up to them. If you try it too early, it can ruin your feet and legs. I've been dancing on point for a couple of years now. That's what I'm going to do when I get back," I say.

"Well I'm going to get back into my music," Katie says.

"What do you do?" I ask.

"I sing, play guitar, and write songs. I was following that band around for a reason; it wasn't only the guitar player. I thought they could help me get on stage. It didn't happen, but it could have."

"So that was the reason for the Mohawk? A kinda stage costume?"

"Yeah, I thought I might get some attention with it, and maybe somebody would give my music a chance, but what happened was, they treated me like a freak and wouldn't even listen to me play. I was going to get rid of it, but then these guys kinda took care of that."

You did look pretty strange with the green dye and all, I'm thinking, *another lesson in hasty judgment.*

"I'm pretty sure if I didn't have the Mohawk when my parents caught up with me, I wouldn't have ended up here, but I think the whole scene freaked them out."

"What kinda songs do you write?" Chastity asks.

"They're sorta folk and sorta protest about what's goin' on in the world."

"Well sing us one," I say.

"Yeah come on, we want to hear one," Chastity says.

"All right," she says. "I'll sing one I call, 'Danny's Downfall'. I named it after one of the kids on the bus who couldn't stay away from alcohol."

When she starts to sing, Katie has a sweet sensuous voice. She slaps her thigh with her open palm, and we all join in with a hand clap to keep the beat. The music in her voice rouses me to get up, and I start dancing as she sings.

Sheriff changin' all the locks, an the keys to Danny's door
Kids are crying, Danny's lyin', Ma can't take it anymore.
Danny's busted, can't be trusted, ain't no jobs and it ain't funny
Nasty people keep on callin', everybody wants their money.

Can't recall when lost it all, sudden fall, it's all a mystery
Never mine, we'll all be fine, cuz we're a savin' up for whiskey.

We all laugh at the chorus, and I dance in a circle around the group. I kick off my desert boots and begin spinning and stepping barefoot to Katie's hand jive beat.

Wall street suits all get the bonus, now they're dinin'- out an drinkin'
Company's broke, makes no difference, they'll be fine, but we're all sinkin'
Wishin' hopin', just ain't workin', gonna work on, his plan B
Danny's hangin', at the shelter, an' he's savin' up for whiskey

Can't recall when lost it all, sudden fall, it's all a mystery
Never mine, we'll all be fine, cuz we're a savin' up for whiskey.

I do some pirouettes and a sad try at a leap. Jordan, Chastity, and I applaud Katie, and they laugh at me. We're all smiles, but it makes me think about home and everything I'm missing back there—and how crazy it is to be singing and dancing out in the scrub brush. Our girls' club ends suddenly when I look up and see Travis returning with the boys. I point them out to the others, and even Jordan looks disappointed that we have to go back to our regimentation.

"What's going on here?" Travis asks.

"We're done with the hair washing, Travis, and we've got a pot of water on the fire if you guys want to use it to clean up," Jordan says.

Travis picks up the pot and spills it on the fire. We all scramble back to escape the smoke and steam cloud.

"Sam and Jimmy take down that enclosure and use the tarps to make a group shelter. Katie and Chastity, help them erect the shelter. Kevin and Julia, clean up this fire mess. I want it to look like it's never been here. Then make a fire ring over there," he points to a spot ten feet away, "and collect enough firewood to make a fire for dinner."

Jordan doesn't say anything. Travis keeps at us the whole time, picking at the way they make the shelter, making them take it down, and rebuild it three times until he gets tired of it and leaves them alone. Then he comes at me and Kevin, kicking the fire pit we made and making us rebuild it the way he thinks it should be.

When he's harassing the others, Kevin whispers to me. "Boy, was he mad when he heard Katie singing. Didn't you guys see us coming back? He flipped out when we got close enough to see you dancing around them. What an asshole."

"What's the big deal, so we had a little fun?"

"I feel sorry for Jordan. He's madder at her than he is at you guys."

"She doesn't deserve that." I say.

"Yeah, but what can she do about it?"

"Maybe we can..."

"What are you two talking about?" Travis says. He comes back to us and scatters our fire pit again with his boots. "Make it bigger and I want it perfectly round and I want more wood."

When Travis gets tired of showing us how nasty he can be, we settle down to a quiet dinner. Jordan has us all write something in our journals. I find I actually have some thoughts to put down.

I love looking at the clear sky during a sunset. It's so peaceful and quiet. It makes everything feel okay for a moment. It all comes together and makes sense. I had a rough day, but I feel I came around. I was sick and feeling really emotional. I hate it when I get that way. I look back and feel kinda stupid because there really wasn't much to be upset about until Travis came back and went nuts. Katie's song and my funny dance were a good break. Mail from my parents gave me a lot to think about. I have a three page letter going back to them. I hope to get a letter from my sister soon. Her letters always cheer me up. The hair washing helped, but I am excited that they promised full body hygiene this week. I feel so dirty and gross.

Gosh, I think about all the bad things and stuff gone wrong. The sky has a pink haze all around, and I look at it and can't be mad. I am a little worried about my "situation," but there is nothing I can do about it now so I am trying not to think about it. I don't know what I would do if I'm pregnant, but I really don't think so and really hope that I'm not. I am figuring out more stuff to work on, like listening to details and being more aware of them. I would also like to work on keeping motivated twenty-four-seven instead of most of the time. I would probably get a lot more done. Things are okay, everything happens for a reason. I know when I am ready and things are all in place I will be home. I will make it.

I don't write in my journal about the little grudge I've developed for Travis and the idea growing in my mind about what to do about it.

***

Dr. Miller drives up at sunrise. It's already stifling. We're all sleeping in our clothes on top of our bags when we hear the van stop and the door slam. The heat weighs on me, lying there wide awake. When Travis goes out to meet him, I follow right behind. I'm looking forward to another conversation with a real human being. The van doesn't have air conditioning by the look of the beads on Miller's forehead; sweat pours down his face even though he's dressed for the weather. Boy, does he look funny. He wears a blue tank top that's one size too small. It stretches tight across his man-boobs and a dark spot in the middle is stuck to his belly. His khaki knee length shorts do a bad job of covering his fat hairy legs that end in a pair of Jesus sandals. I try not to look at the ugly fungus on his big toe nail. The oddest part is, when you look at him above the neck, there's the head of a mature, bearded psychologist sitting on top of this cartoon of a body. He's breathing hard like big people do when they get hot, and he carries a big thermos and a paper bag rolled up at the top.

"Brought you some coffee and bagels. Don't worry Travis. It's nothing off the diet."

"Thanks, David," Travis says. "It will be nice to have coffee where you don't have to chew the grounds."

Travis unscrews the top of the thermos, pours coffee in it, and hands it to Dr. Miller. Then he poured himself a cup. When I hold out my cup, he turns away and sets the thermos down without a word. Dr. Miller picks up the thermos and pours me some.

"Julia, we'll talk right after breakfast. I'm anxious to hear how you're getting along."

"Thanks, Dr. Miller."

I know enough to take the coffee and walk away before Travis has a chance to hit me with one of his condescending commands.

The rest of the camp gets up, and we go about our regular morning chores and get our breakfast. Dr. Miller sets up some chairs in the little bit of shade the van makes and calls me over.

"So what's new?"

I try to look mostly at his face when I talk to him. I want to talk to the psychologist not the cartoon. I tell him about the lightning storm, the fire, and the electric-light spider on the ground. He asks me if anybody got hurt, and I tell him we were all saved because Mark knew what to do. He makes notes on his yellow legal pad. I'm glad the pad covers up his pudgy legs.

"Doesn't anybody tell you what happens out here?" I ask.

"Nobody said anything about that. What else?"

That's when I go into the coyote story, and he really gets to scribbling then.

"Anything else?" I could tell he was hoping I would say no.

"Only a lot of boring hikes and lots of time to think."

"What are you thinking about?"

"I'm worried I might be pregnant. I didn't take any precautions the first couple of times, but then I got some pills. It's been a while since I had a period. It really worries me."

"You're OK, Julia. You were tested when you first came into the program. You are not pregnant."

"Whew, that's a relief, but what about the missed periods?"

"It happens a lot because of the physical stress and diet change. Don't worry about it."

The sun moves around the edge of the van, and I move my chair to get back in the shade.

"What else are you thinking about?"

"Home. My family. What I have to do to get out of here."

"Well, you should know that I get good reports on you, and everybody recognizes that you are working with the program. How's it going with the fire-making?"

"It's so hard. I can do it, but as soon as I think I have the perfect set-up, something always breaks."

"You know that's the lesson, don't you?"

"Yeah, I get it, but it's frustrating. Still, I know I can do it now so the setbacks aren't so bad. At first, I didn't think I would ever be able to do it and that scared me. Now I get it. Fear of failure only gets in the way of doing a thing but knowing that you have to find a way can get you over the fear."

"Well said, Julia." He had a warm smile when he was pleased. "How are things going with the letters?"

At least he remembered my complaint about my dad's nagging.

"I know you must have said something to my dad because he quit trying to work me over about the past and my friends and is sending me newsy stuff instead. They're working on my room for when I get back home. At least I know they haven't moved and changed their names so they never have to see me again."

"Hey, quit feeling sorry for yourself. You're going to get through this fine, and you'll be back in the family before you know it."

"You know, right now, that's all I want. It took a big shock to show me, but my mom and dad and sister are the only people I need in my life. The rest of people in this world are not nearly as important."

"Do you need any spiritual support?"

"You mean a preacher or somethin'? God, no. I'm an atheist."

"So you don't think there's a higher spirit that can explain the mystery of how the universe works?"

"Look, my dad can explain the mystery of how a TV works, but that doesn't make him God. Let's move on OK?"

"Right. Julia, unless there is something else you want to talk about, we should wrap this up. I need to spend time with the others."

"Fine with me. Thanks for talking with me, Dr. Miller. There is one other thing. You know people pretty well. I mean you are kind of in touch with personalities, right?"

"That's my business."

"You don't think Travis would get aggressive with Jordan, do you?"

"What? Aggressive how? What do you mean?"

"Nothing, never mind, it's nothing." I get up and put out a hand to shake. "Forget I said it."

He gives me his hand and looks at me like he wants to question me. I turn around so he won't see the smile I can't contain and walk off. People say they can feel people watching them. I feel him watching me walk away.

***

We stay in camp for three days. Dr. Miller spends time with each of us. He's good to talk to. I keep working on my bow drill kit. Getting fires is the only way to advance, and I sure as hell want to advance to going home. Travis keeps telling me everything I'm doing wrong; his instructions help, but I hate his attitude.

"That is the worst spindle I have ever seen anyone trying to use. Why don't you throw the whole kit away and start over?"

"What am I doing wrong, Travis? I do want to get this right. Can't you help me?"

He puffs up and takes my stuff, going through it piece by piece and telling me what's wrong with all of it. I listen attentively.

"So Travis, are you and Jordan—you know?" I say as we work.

"What are you talking about? Never mind, keep working on this."

He takes the piece I'm shaving and begins working it slowly with his pocket knife.

"You know. Everybody sees the way she looks at you when you aren't looking."

The knife starts working faster.

"What do you mean?" he says. I can almost hear the wheels spinning in his so-called brain.

"Don't you know she's attracted to you?"

He goes silent at that. More gears meshing. I looked for steam coming out of his ears.

"Never mind Julia," he says, but I can tell he's absorbed my message like a dry sponge thrown in a bucket of water. He hands me the piece, stands abruptly, and walks off with an odd, dreamy expression.

***

We break camp the next day. It takes us 'til noon to pack up and make it look like nobody has ever been there. When it's done to Travis' satisfaction, Jordan leads out with me, Chastity, and Katie. The boys follow with Travis at the rear of the line. We walk for two hours at a time, taking short breaks, then going on again. It's a cloudy day, which keeps it from getting too hot. About mid afternoon we can see and hear a thunderstorm off to the north, maybe twenty miles away. We can see the vertical lines of the rain fall from black clouds, but it never comes at us, though I keep worrying we could get it. I'm still a little nervous after that last one.

We stop at a barren place, no trees or nothing. Jordan hands out some protein bars, and when she gives one to Travis, I catch his eye and wink at him. I see the hint of a smile, but he vanishes it right away. I watch him try to get a conversation going with Jordan, but she kind of ignores him. She goes about making sure everybody's drinking enough water and adjusts packs that need tightening up.

When we make camp that night, Travis is all energized about making up the shelter, and at the cook fire, he makes up a hot chocolate for Jordan who takes it with a little surprised "thank you" which makes Travis puff up again.

When it comes time to write in our journals, I rip out the last page in my notebook and tear a piece off. I burn the rest of the page in the fire. On the torn piece, I write a short note in my best cursive.

"Meet after they're asleep. Burn this. J."

When it's time to crawl into our bags, I drop the folded-up note into Travis' empty cup and watch for him to find it. We push the fire together before we go to sleep, and I work with Travis to cover it with cow patties to keep the coals alive for breakfast cooking in the morning.

I see him find the note. He looks around to see if anyone notices, unfolds the paper, reads it, smiles, looks over at Jordan, and puts it in the fire. I'm thoroughly enjoying myself. Darla would have been proud of me. I slip into my sleeping bag and wait.

We all sleep in one shelter that night. Two of our biggest tarps are bound together to make what looks like a huge pup tent. Boys on one side, feet to the middle, girls on the other, same way. Travis has his bag at one of the open ends, and Jordan has hers at the other.

The moon must be on the other side of the planet because the night is black as coal and that makes it easy to fall asleep after the long hike. I try to fight off sleep, but I drift in and out. After an hour or so, the sounds of sleep-breathing make it clear that everybody has faded. I'd be laughing at some of the dream mumbles I hear, but I don't want to let on I'm still awake. Kevin is the most active. He keeps going on about his mother.

"Mom, oh mom, stay with me, please let me stay."

It's sad to listen to him. Then Travis stirs. I can't see him, but I hear him get up and walk around the outside of the tent. He must be barefoot because I hear him swear at stepping on something in the dark. He comes around to Jordan's end of the tent, and I can make out a vague silhouette against the star-lit sky. I can't see exactly what happens, but I think he bends down over Jordan to kiss her because the next thing I hear is this terrified scream.

Jordan jumps up and knocks Travis flat on his back. He scrambles back up.

"Oh my God! What do you think you're doing?" she screams.

"But I thought..." Travis comes toward Jordan.

"You have no right, Travis. Get away from me!"

By this time, the whole tent is awake and gaping at the two counselors.

"Are you crazy? First of all, I never gave you any reason to think..."

"But the note..."

"What note?"

"The note that said to come to you tonight."

"You are out of your mind—I didn't give you any note. Where is this note?"

"I burned it like you said."

"Travis, get away from me. Don't you ever touch me again. I've had it with you. You're rude, you're mean and now this. We are done. I'm calling for a replacement first thing in the morning. One of us is going, you or me. I don't care which, but we're done."

"But Julia..."

"Don't you dare bring any of the kids into this, Travis..."

"Now Jordan, I'm sorry, it was a mistake, I don't know what happened. I thought—you know."

"No I don't know. You can do whatever you want, but I will be wide awake the rest of the night, and you'd better stay away from me."

"What's going on?" Jimmy D. starts to get up.

"Stay there Jimmy. Everybody go back to sleep. It's OK," says Jordan.

"Jordan, I want to..."

"Don't talk to me, Travis. Get away from me. Now!"

Travis returns to his end of the tent. Jordan sits up at hers.

In the morning, Jordan makes a call, and within an hour, the white van comes with Mark and Amy—and leaves with Travis. We never see Travis again.

Slow days pass by
I count them
As I cry.
The long awaited
Day gets near
When I will finally
Be out of here.

CHAPTER 26

JULIA

Some people say keeping a secret means telling people one at a time, but I know enough to keep my mouth shut tight about what I did to Travis. I don't say nothin' to nobody. I don't feel the need to brag about it because there is plenty of satisfaction in what happened. I worry a little about running into him again sometime because I know he'll figure out it was me that did him, but I put that worry aside for another day and enjoy the fact that the whole atmosphere changes after he leaves.

I realize I've settled in to my new life. It had been hard at first, when everything was all new. I didn't know anybody and didn't know what to expect, but after awhile, I get some confidence and know I can get through. The unknowns are replaced with routine, and all the weird stuff gets familiar. I learn the system and begin to feel comfortable working it.

The hikes aren't so tough for me anymore. In the beginning, it killed me to do two miles with a fifty-pound pack. The other day we hiked eight miles, and I carried sixty pounds with no problem. I'm always hiking really fast too. I've gotten so strong out here it's unbelievable. The hikes are like nothing. I carry sixty-five-pound water jugs a quarter mile from water drop up to camp.

I finally catch on to the bow drilling thing. I know they have us doing it to keep us busy, but I've fallen for the challenge. It's kinda like learning to ride a bicycle—you don't think you'll ever get it. You keep falling down, skinning your knees, and scraping your elbows until one day you figure it out. Then you're off and running.

I can bow drill a fire like nothing. They keep count, and I've made seventeen fires. Me and Jimmy D. have become the group's instructors on bow drilling when a new kid arrives.

The desert is a familiar setting for me now. There's a peaceful beauty to the place with its long distance views and simple landscape. We see coyotes lots of times; they're really shy and stay away from us, not like those other ones on my solo. Mostly, we hear them at night, howling in the distance. I always stay awake until they've stopped. The only other big animals we see are the antelope. Mark says they're not really antelope, they're pronghorns. They're only three feet tall and have funny looking horns that curl in toward each other, and they run in herds. You should see them go when we scare them sometimes. Mark says they can outrun a coyote.

***

One day after a long hike, we make camp at a place they call Tweetie. I always wonder where in the hell they come up with these names. We've been here a couple of days, waiting for a supply run when the white van shows up with water and food. It also brings Victoria.

She's a psychologist like Dr. Miller, and I have a session with her. It's probably because she's a woman, but I feel more comfortable with her than I did with David.

"Julia, I'm here instead of Dr. Miller today. He thought it might be good for you to have a woman to talk to this time. How are you getting along?"

She seems more organized than he was. She sets up one of those umbrella canopies and a couple of chairs for us.

"Are you a psychologist too?"

"Yes, I am, and Dr. Miller filled me in on you and your progress. You're getting along pretty well according to him."

"I'm ready to go home."

"Let's talk about that, OK."

This is the first time anyone has agreed to talk about getting me out of here.

"I'm willing."

"We're going to have to get into some detail about why you're here in the first place and what's going to be different when you do go home."

Miller was right. It does feel good to talk to a woman. She's a lot like him in her matter-of-fact ways, but still, she's different in ways that make it easier.

"You want the dirty laundry?" I ask.

"You might call it that."

"You guys have my diary; you already know most of it."

"We need to go over it, tell me."

"I guess I'm glad to have it all out in the open, not hanging on my shoulders. Truthfully some of the things in that diary I had forgotten about. Anyway here it goes. I had sex with the three people I wrote about, and there was no one else. And for the record, I really wasn't doing anything in the hot tub with Mike, Darla, and Johnny. I was exposed to an STD but wasn't diagnosed with it. I went to the doctor and everything. I drank on occasion, two or three times a month, depending. I smoked cigarettes and pot. I smoked a lot of pot. I've done shrooms twice. I might have done crack, I don't know. I smoked pot laced with something once, maybe crack, that's what we guessed it to be. I have also done one other drug only once; it was maybe meth, but I don't know. I didn't pop pills except once, and it wasn't a narcotic pill, I don't think. I have obviously skipped school and gotten bad grades. I usually rode the bus to Ashland and hung out on the street or went to the orchards and smoked pot. I have snuck out of the house on several occasions to go party or see Mike. This only started like a month and a half before I came here. I have been smoking pot since seventh grade. The first people I smoked with were Ellie Smith, Darla, and Maggie. I don't know if you want specific circumstances. I could go on for days; this is an overall. I don't even remember all the exact times and places for all the stupid things I've done. This is the worst of it. When I ran away, I partied but was safe—and didn't do anything completely stupid. I don't even remember now. I couch hopped a lot, and one night I slept in a friend's car with Ellie in front of their house. I'm not holding back anything, so if anything new comes up, I will be glad to acknowledge it. The only reason I didn't tell you is because I forgot. So, I'll leave this my dirt list."

"Do you have any idea why your parents might have sent you here?" she said, leaning over in her chair and looking me straight in the eye.

"Yeah—I get it."

"Julia, you must know how dangerous methamphetamine is. You're a smart girl."

"I wasn't going to do it until my front teeth fell out."

"Nobody is ever planning to do it until their teeth fall out. It's an addiction. You can get addicted by doing it only once. It's a terribly destructive drug."

I'm glad she isn't shaking her finger at me, but she doesn't really need to.

"I know that, but we get tired of having adults try to scare us with bullshit. When we rebel, we want to show them that they're wrong. They lie to us about how bad pot is, but we know better. When they tell us the truth about how bad methamphetamine is, maybe we don't believe them or take it seriously."

"It's bad. Believe it. Don't ever do it again," she says.

"OK, I got it. I know. I was being contrary. I won't."

"What do you think your parents could have done other than send you here?"

Victoria has my number. She knows it, and I know it. We're tuned to the same channel. I take a deep breath before I respond.

"Nothing."

Victoria looks at me with a huge smile. "Julia, my dear, you have had a breakthrough."

"I know."

"How do you feel?"

"Relieved. Thankful. Stupid. Better."

"OK. Let's put it all in perspective. You made some mistakes, and everybody is ready to forgive you. Now you have to forgive yourself, and you have to forgive your parents. It's time to restart your life. We're not talking about starting over; you need to pick up from when you made the wrong turn and move on. Now listen carefully, Julia. You are not your past—you are who you are today, and who you will be in the future. Are you ready for that?"

I don't know why it gets to me right at that moment, but I start to cry. All the tension built up in me forces me to start, and I can't stop. Victoria comes over to me, puts her soft arms around me, and holds me close there for a long time. I let it go on. I don't try to stop, I keep crying until it's over. I cry so hard my face is wet, and I get the hiccips, like when I was a little kid and can't catch my breath. It feels so good. Her arms make it easy, and when I finally stop, I look up at Victoria. She has tears in her eyes too.

Victoria pulls out some tissue, and we both wipe our eyes. When Victoria blows her nose with a honk that sounds like the call of the geese we see sometimes, we hold our breath and look at each other until we can't contain a laugh explosion that bends her over and shakes me from head to toe.

"Hey, I think we're going to be OK. How about you?" she says as she wipes the tears from her cheeks.

I sniffle and nod, still trying to catch my breath from the crying and the laughing and the hiccuping.

"Let's go for a little walk," she says.

"OK," I say, hiccup again. We both laugh, and she hands me another tissue.

We walked away from the camp in silence until we both get composed before turning back.

"I think it's time for lunch," Victoria says.

"I'm starving," I agree.

CHAPTER 27

STEVEN

Victoria called me and Mary on a Friday night.

"Hold on," she said. "Mr. Edelman is going to join us on the call."

"Is everything OK with Julia?" Mary asked.

"She's doing great—Oh, here's Mr. Edelman now."

There were a few clicks and a buzz on the line, then...

"Hello Steven and Mary, this is the call you've been waiting for. Julia is ready to come home."

"Are you sure?" asked Mary, "We really can't go through the runaway business again."

"We've done what we can, she's still a teenager. You're still going to have to keep a close watch on her, but she's come to some realizations. I know you'll find it easier to get along with her if you implement our program. All you have to do is follow the suggestions in my book— it's all laid out there—and I'm sure you'll be fine."

"How soon can we come get her?" I asked.

All I could think about was having my daughter back home and my family together again. I felt a narcotic-like jolt diffuse my blood stream, followed by a calming sedation embodied in the realization we were reaching the summit of a long hard climb.

"We have a little ceremony for this. We plan it as a surprise for Julia, with a transitional picnic to allow everyone to get used to each other again before you pack her up and take her home," he said. "Can you come to Bend next weekend for the event?"

"You bet. Give us a place and time, and we'll be there," I said.

And so it was arranged. We would be one of three families coming to retrieve their teenager. We were warned not to spill the beans to Julia; the surprise was part of it, but I got the feeling they wanted to avoid the consequence of having known short-timers in contact with the other kids.

***

We met at the wilderness school offices. Kevin's mother was there for him, both Chastity's parents came, and me and Mary and Bree.

Kevin's mother was Eva, who was two hours late and no apology. She insisted her name be pronounced "AY-VAH." I guessed Ay-vah to be around thirty. She was perfectly groomed in a high fashion sort of way, medium length hair that had been cut so well it fell naturally without a curl out of place. Her long fingers were flawlessly manicured and lacquered. She wore tailored blue jeans that fit perfectly to flatter a figure that needed no flattering and a cowboy cut, pearl button shirt that still had fold creases betraying the fact it was purchased for the occasion. The shirt was tucked into the jeans over a flat stomach, and an expensive looking leather belt with a silver buckle was a close match for her Rodeo Drive cowboy boots. Eva appeared to be happy with herself and didn't need to participate in any conversation with us or the other parents. She was there to perform a duty and was going to be relieved when it was over. She had other things to do. She was attractive and she knew it.

Jim and Gena were Chastity's parents. They were unpretentious and friendly. Jim had a hard time keeping his eyes off Eva, but so did I. They had started early that morning and driven up from Sacramento, almost eight hours to get to Bend. They were a little weary, but anxious to see their daughter again. We chatted while we waited for the staff to get things ready for our meeting. Mary kept Gena in conversation. Jim told me he was an attorney—family trusts, probates, LLCs and that stuff, nothing nasty. He was probably forty or so, but the shaved head and lack of any facial hair gave him a youthful look. He was as anxious to get his daughter back as I was for Julia. When he told me how hard it was for him to make the decision to send her to the school, I felt I had met a kindred spirit.

Gena was pretty in a girl-next-door, fresh, healthy sort of way. Her glittering long blonde hair framed a face with a rosy, baby smooth complexion. She wore a flower print sun dress that only added to the fresh-as-a-daisy impression she made. The long early morning car trip hadn't diminished her natural energies or dampened her obvious joy at the coming reunion.

We were assembled in an informal classroom in the same building where we'd brought Julia three months before. We sat through a briefing before we left for the campground. The gist of it was we were being given a second chance with our child. We needed to be strong and watchful, and it was going to be all up to us from here on. I didn't like being lectured to again, and my mind kept wandering back and forth between the briefing charts and the peek-a-boo gap between the second and third pearl buttons of Eva's shirt. I was sure she wasn't wearing a bra.

Around noon, we all got into our cars and caravanned out to a wooded recreation area about forty minutes south. We parked and walked a hundred yards to a campground where we waited for the kids to come. They were hiking—unknowing—along a trail where they would pass a hundred feet from where we hid, each of us behind a tall cedar, waiting for their arrival.

When I saw them walking up the trail together, I ran out to meet Julia, picked her up off the ground, and spun around with her in my arms, pack and all. I don't know what the others did. Mary and Bree came up, and I put Julia back down and helped her take off her pack. We all hugged. The surprise and shock was evident on Julia's face. We were all stunned at our reunion.

I looked over my daughter from head to foot. Julia was different. She was filled out and tanned. We had sent-out a pale ballerina and got a woodsy girl back. It didn't matter, I felt so relieved. No more thoughts about what she was doing. She seemed shy toward us. The sudden change of circumstance would buffet anyone, and she was trying to process it. The physical reunion felt like a great first step in getting our daughter back. I didn't expect her to be changed because I knew Julia was still the strong-willed person she had always been. No, she wasn't changed, but she had been forcefully counseled—and I hoped some of it had gotten through to her. This whole thing hadn't been about breaking her spirit. It was more about getting her attention and having our side of the story told.

I thought some of it would sink in right away, but I knew some of it would take awhile. The wall hadn't come down entirely, but we had broken a few chinks in it. We were going to work those for all they were worth.

The staff had prepared a graduation ceremony which was really unnecessary, but we accepted it for the formality that it was and heard it out. Then there was a lunch, camp style, hot dogs and chips. For the vegetarian Julia, no big deal, but the meat eaters, Kevin and Chastity, dug in.

Chastity's mother couldn't stop preening her daughter. She'd brought a change of clothes, and it wasn't long before Chastity was dressed in a pair of white dungarees, a blousy shirt, and low heels. Her mother worked her over with a hairbrush and scented hand towels. Jim looked a little left out but didn't seem to mind not being part of the girly preparations. Chastity loved the attention and couldn't stop smiling, pleased that her ordeal was over.

Kevin got talkative while we ate. He told us all about how to bow drill a fire and offered to show us, but his gear wasn't in the best of shape—and he finally gave up. His mother stayed quiet through the whole thing, and I noticed Julia looking her over several times. When Eva asked for the way to the restrooms, Amy gave her directions, and Julia offered to go with her.

After they walked away, Mary said to me, "She put on quite a bit of weight out here didn't she?"

"Must have been all that hiking and the high protein diet," I said.

"Well I hope she can get back to dance weight soon."

"Mary, that is the least consideration for me. We have her back. We've broken the chain of dissolution, and we're a family again. That's what counts for me."

"I know you're right," Mary said. "I only have to get used to her again."

"We all do. How about you, Bree?"

"I think she's going to be OK, Dad," Bree answered. "I agree with you. It's great to have my sister back."

Unknown futures
Forgettable pasts
Cherished presents
Nothing lasts

CHAPTER 28

JULIA

We hike all morning on a trail we've never taken before. Kevin and Chastity and I hike alone, which seems strange after being under the thumb of the control freaks for so long. They tell us it's a group solo, and we're supposed to hike three miles to the river and set up camp there. They give us enough food for the day, and we carry enough water to last two or three days. We talk as we walk along.

"I think it's a test," Kevin says. "They're probably watching us right now with binoculars or tracking us with infra-red sensors or something."

"Let's be smart about this and do as we're told," I say. "I'm tired of this whole thing and the last thing I want to do is get another setback in my program. All they ever want to do is prevent us from ever getting out of here."

"Yeah, I'm with you, Julia, and Kevin's probably right too. They're setting us up for something and waiting for us to mess up," Chastity says.

"Well, keep your voices down. We're not supposed to talk while we hike," I say.

"You know what, Julia, that is bull—shit. There's nobody around, and I'm not so scared of them I won't talk to you guys," Kevin says.

"Fine, but don't talk too loud, OK?" I say.

It's right about then that my eye catches some movement in the woods, and this guy jumps out from behind a tree. It's my dad grabbing me and picking me up off the ground. Then there are people everywhere, and I know it's over. My mom and my sister come and hug me, and it feels great. I don't know what to say. I'm not mad at them anymore, but I can't adjust to having them all around me again right away.

"Hey, Sister, I've been missin' you, you little brat," Bree says. She has that big smile for me, the one that always makes you know she means it. "You look like you put on some muscle, girl."

"Oh yeah, wanna arm wrestle? You don't know how much I missed you guys," I tell her and hug her again.

"What do you want to do first?" my dad asks me. I look at his face, the face I couldn't remember. He seems older, maybe a few grey hairs in his sideburns.

It's a good question. I hadn't given it any thought, but it doesn't take long to zero in on the material things I miss the most. "I want a long hot shower and a bubble bath followed by an hour in the hot tub." Then I lean over and whisper in my sister's ear "with a joint and a cold beer."

"I'm sure we can arrange all of that once we get back to the house," Bree says and winks at me.

My dad picks up my pack. I think the weight surprises him because he stumbles a little bit before he straightens up. We start over to where a picnic is set out on a table. My mom puts her arm around my waist as we walk.

"Julia, I know this has been hard for you. I hope you and I can start over."

I stop and kiss her cheek. "It's all right, Mom. We're gonna be OK, you and me."

She hugs me then, and we hurry to catch up with the others. I look around for Kevin and Chastity. Kevin is already at the picnic table digging into a bag of chips; his mother is sitting on the bench next to him looking bored. Chastity's mother is at her with a hairbrush, and her dad is showing Amy how to operate their camera for a group shot.

I feel frozen in time, somewhere between the past and the future. Both strike me as unreal. The present is dream-like. I don't know what to do with myself. Like I have a new-found freedom, but I'm stuck by the glue of habit to the regimented trail life I've been living. I'm proud of myself for getting through— it kinda proves I didn't need them to get by—but at the same time, I want to be with them.

I'd dreamed of this day. They have a corny ceremony. Adults are always having corny ceremonies. I sit through it quietly thinking about everything that's happened, then about my old friends, then what was going to happen to Kevin. His mom seems like a bitch all dressed up like some kinda Beverly Hills cowgirl, and she hardly even speaks to him or anyone else either. Chastity looks like she's in her element with her mom fussing over her like that, so Chastity is going to be fine. It's Kevin that I wonder about, so when his mother goes off to find the potties, I follow her.

"Hi, are you Kevin's mom?" I ask, catching up to her on the foot path to the bath house.

"Who are you?" she says to me over her shoulder.

"I'm Julia. Kevin and I got to know each other here in the wilderness school."

She stops walking and turns to look at me, then spins around again and starts walking away.

"Oh, so you're the girl that he talked about in those letters."

She's walking away and talking like I don't deserve to have her full attention.

"Yes, I am. He wrote you quite a few letters but didn't get many back."

"I've been busy."

"He actually only got one letter from you the whole time I knew him."

"I've been busy."

"What have you been doing?" I ask.

"Listen, Julia," she stops walking and turns to me and looks me up and down. "I don't have to answer to a twelve-year-old girl. It's none of your business what I do. I'm busy."

"I'm fifteen, and I'm Kevin's friend, and I don't think you are very nice to him. He's a very lonely boy, and he needs his family to pay attention to him and love him."

"If I wanted your opinion about my son, I'd ask for it. And just to be clear, I don't want to hear anymore opinions from a rude and sassy little juvenile delinquent bitch like you." She turns and walks away fast.

I yell at her back, "Right, your highness, just thought I'd let you know."

I don't think what I say to her makes any difference, but it feels good to say it. I'm glad I made her mad.

It gives me a feeling of power to spin up an adult like that. One that really deserves it. I don't follow her to the toilets but turn around and go back to the picnic. I go right up to my mom and kiss her on the cheek. I then kiss the bald spot on the back of my dad's head. They look surprised, but I know they like it. I want to thank them for all the letters they wrote to me, but I don't know how to say it.

A battle between
My mind and heart
My mind makes for a better start
My heartaches sting along the way
I will find peace
It will come to stay

CHAPTER 29

JULIA

When I get back home, it feels like a luxury vacation. I have a new room, freshly painted, and they've set up a waterbed for me. It's a little retro, but I love it. I take advantage of sleeping as long as I want, watch hours of TV, and eat whatever I want whenever I want it. I spend hours re-organizing my wardrobe.

The first time I look at myself naked in a full-length mirror, I'm shocked at how filled out I am. My usual vegan diet doesn't have anything like the protein I ate on the trail, so it doesn't take long for the bulk to go away and my dancer body to show up again.

They have rules for me, but they aren't too tough. The hardest thing— I'm not supposed to even talk to my old friends. There's one girlfriend they like, Maggie, and I'm allowed to talk to her, which is where I get all the news on everybody else.

Maggie doesn't know much about Mike, except that he's still hanging around the high school picking up freshman girls and living in the same house on Plum Street. She doesn't know anything about the other boys at all. Our closest girlfriends, Darla and Simone, have been busy. Darla is two months pregnant and planning to get married. Simone's real-dad tricked her into flying out to his house in Montana for a week vacation, but when she got there, he told her she couldn't go back, that her mom couldn't deal with her anymore. Maggie asks me how I liked the long letters she sent me when I was away. When I tell her I never got any letters from her, she gets really mad at Bree.

I don't want to go back to school. I want to get a GED, but my dad says I have to finish high school—and that is that. Edelman told me when I left the wilderness school that my parents could send me back there for free if I went back to my old habits so I go along with the high school thing. They get a friend to let them use their address in Ashland and register me for Ashland High. They won't let me go back to the old school where all the trouble started. I have about a month before school to get adjusted.

When school starts, I take a city bus into Ashland. The bus stop is like three miles from our house, so my dad drives me every morning to the stop on his way to work. We wait in the car until we see the bus coming. I have to listen to the news on the public radio station. If I try to talk to him over the news, he always starts asking me questions, but he can't pin me down too hard on a five-minute drive.

"Don't you ever have homework Julia? I never see you doing any homework."

"I get it done on the bus, Dad. It's forty-five minutes each way; there's nothing else to do on the bus. I sure don't want to talk to the creeps on there." If he gets too nosy, my out is always, "I see the bus, gotta go."

***

My mom and I kinda make up. Since I don't have any friends and she doesn't have a job, we hang out together. She takes me shopping for school clothes, and I help her with the grocery shopping. I have the feeling she isn't so sure about me—I mean that I've changed. The one good thing is she lets the past go; she doesn't grind me about it.

***

When school starts, I'm by myself. I don't have any friends at the high school, so when I get free time, I usually walk through downtown, looking in the store windows and watching bored tourists wandering around, waiting for the next theatre performance or lining up at one of the fancy restaurants that I can never afford.

I meet Blake the first time at the town plaza during my lunch hour. He sits cross-legged on the sidewalk in front of the candy shop, strumming a guitar. The case is open in front of him with a few seed coins in it. He's sorta little like me in physical build; I mean no extra flesh on skinny bones and short for a guy. He has dreadlocks, tied in a bandana, and wears white muslin pants and a tee shirt. It's a costume that says, "I don't give a damn about the establishment. I'm goin' my own way, and I don't need any of their bullshit." He has brazen blue eyes and is clean shaven, although I'm not sure he even has to shave. The best overall description of him is that he is kind of effeminate, and he has an aura about him that makes you want to take care of him. Like he needs you, but he's independent too.

"Anything you wanna hear?" he asks me as I walk by.

I stop and turn to see him grinning at me and walk back. "What can you play?" He has a nice smile, and I like having someone to talk to.

"I can play almost anything you know the words to. I only know three chords, C, G and D, but they're the one's you need to play most songs. Try me."

"*What I Got* by Sublime."

"You got it."

He starts to play and sing. "Early in the morning, risin' to the street, light me up that cigarette and I strap shoes on my feet..."

He knows all the words, and he isn't too bad a singer. I listen while he sings it to me. When he's done, I throw a bus token in his guitar case and start to walk away.

"Hey girl, what's your name?"

"Julia, what's yours?"

"Blake, see you around, OK?"

I meet him a couple of times after that, down at the plaza, and it takes off from there. Sometimes we smoke a joint in the park before I go back to school. It isn't any big deal. Nobody hassles you in Ashland. There are three classes of people in the town: college students riding their parents' savings or their student loans, retired rich people with nothing to do but go to restaurants and theatre, and the high school crowd that ends up waiting tables and pumping gas for everybody else. Nobody cares if you smoke a joint in the park. Eventually, he invites me to his apartment—and I go.

***

When I return to the dance studio, I come with a new attitude. My once lazy, whatever attitude is replaced with a new confidence. I want to be good at it. I know I can be, and I'm willing to do whatever it takes. It feels good to be working out my body with dance instead of carrying sixty-pound packs. Before they sent me away, I only went through the motions. It was something to do. I wasn't serious. When I come back to it, I see it differently. I want to be the best in the studio. There are some older girls who dance well, and I think I can do as well as they do if I work at it. I think I can be better. I had learned I could do some stuff that looked impossible if I seriously work at it, and I apply that lesson to my dance and give it a go.

The dance teacher knows my story. I can feel her reluctance at having me back in the school, a spoiled apple in the bushel. In the past, I'd been one of the regulars who showed up every week for two hours and thought nothing about dance until the next lesson. I'm changed, but she doesn't know it.

"Julia, you're back," Mrs. Roberta Smith says. "Are you going to be a regular again? You know you've missed a lot of practice. I hope you can catch up with the rest of the girls. You've put on a little weight, haven't you?" Her tone is not encouraging; a little condescending. Although she'd never refuse to let me come back, it's clear I'm on probation. We had gotten along pretty well before, but I know this seventy-year-old woman is way over on the conservative side, so her opinion of me is not positive. I accept the challenge.

The studio floor is full of girls ready for their lesson, all dancer-dressed: leotards, tights, and hair buns. I can see them all in the mirror wall, sneaking peeks at me. I'm a topic. Some of them huddle in the far corner of the room where I know they're gossiping about me. Others stand or sit on the floor close to where Roberta and I talk, pretending they aren't listening.

"Yes, Roberta," all the students call her by her first name, "I'm here to dance, and I'm ready to work at it. I want to try out for the solo in the fall recital," I say.

"Oh! There are a lot of girls who've been working hard on that dance while you were gone. It might be hard for you to compete with them."

"It's OK, as long as I have a fair chance at it, I'll do my best."

I know I'm kidding myself about the fair chance. There's politics everywhere, and the dance studio is a hot bed of favoritism, parental influence, and behind-the-scenes scheming. Still, I'm willing to dive into the swamp, wrestle the snakes and sink, or swim, by my own efforts. The new Julia is not going to be a dud.

"Well let's warm up then," she says to the room full of girls, "everybody on the bar."

No one speaks to me, and they give me lots of room at the bar. When I lift my leg up to the waist-high bar, my tight muscles bend me backwards and I let out an involuntary groan. There are giggles coming from the others who stand straight up and effortlessly bend forward to touch their flat bellies to the thighs of their bar-high horizontal legs. I catch Roberta's eye and the hint of a smirk on her lined face. Everything tells me I have a long way to go.

But the muscle bulk slowly disappears, and my dancer frame re-emerges over several weeks. The notoriety of my first days at the studio loses its interest, and the troupe warms up to me little by little, even Roberta.

By the beginning of October, Roberta recognizes my dedication and progress—and offers a little carrot.

"I've been watching you work, Julia. I see that you've been working on the fairy solo from *Sleeping Beauty*. No one else is attempting it. Do you want to do it in the fall show?"

I can't believe my ears. "Yes, of course, I'd love to." She gives me a copy of the Tchaikovsky arrangement for my practice.

When the word gets out, Roberta's offer changes everything for me. The girls start talking to me again, and Roberta's staff works with me on my costume for the performance.

My parents are watching my every move. I can't get to Blake's on the weekends, and I need to get out of the house, so I spend my extra time at the studio. Roberta has no classes on Saturday mornings, so she lets me use the studio when she comes in with her husband to take care of the week's paperwork. Sometimes she gives me one-on-one coaching, and it really pays off. I'm still a little muscle bound and can't do the high kicks the way she wants them, but my feet toughen up again to the toe shoes—and I make the dance mine. I can feel I'm creeping up on the older girls who were the studio stars and begin to feel some jealous tension.

***

The fall recital is on Halloween weekend. My parents have a costume party to attend on the night of my performance. They have never missed any of my performances; they're good about stuff like that. I've gotten over being embarrassed about them, even when they come to the recital in costume. That's the night my dad meets Blake.

My mom is a bit of a Halloween freak. She loves to decorate the house, get dressed up, and go to costume parties. My dad goes along with it for her sake, but he's not really into it. This particular day, she's convinced some of their friends to go to my dance performance before going on to their party. They're all in costume, and it's kind of festive. One of the friends brings a bunny head covering for my dad to wear. It's like a fuzzy pink cap that covers his entire head except for his face, fastens under his chin, and it has long pink ears that stick straight up. Now my dad wears glasses and has a full mustache. He wears his hair kinda long too so it pokes out here and there around the bottom of the cap. He looks ridiculous peering out of the bunny head. I give him an "A" for being a good sport. That's the get-up he has on when he first sees Blake in the audience, and Bree tells him Blake is my new boyfriend. When he finds out Blake is nineteen, that does it.

My dad, in bunny head gear, looking like he stepped out of a poorly cast *Alice in Wonderland* movie, goes up to Blake, "You are not dating my daughter, buddy."

Blake stares at him.

"You're too old for Julia, and I don't want you dating her, get it?"

Blake says nothing.

"Leave her alone," Dad tells him, shakes his finger in his face, makes his meanest bunny-man face and walks away.

I get the story secondhand from Blake. We have a good laugh at Dad's expense when Blake describes the confrontation and how he had a hard time keeping a straight face in front of the six-foot tall bunny-man laying down the law.

My solo goes off flawlessly, my pirouettes get me an applause, and I'll always remember that show as the beginning of my dance comeback.

***

What my dad doesn't know is, I'm taking the early bus into Ashland so I can get off at the stop in front of Blake's apartment building, and hop into bed with him in the morning before school. To be honest, I never would go to school if Blake doesn't insist. He's afraid if I don't go, I'll get in trouble again and have to go back to the wilderness school. So I go to Blake's first, then to school almost every day.

Things go on like this for a couple of months until the morning I have trouble climbing the stairs to Blake's door. It hits me in the stomach like a bad burrito when I step off the bus. I feel weak, sweaty, and so sick I'm afraid I'll vomit in the street. When I get to his apartment, I sit down on the landing, lean against the wall next to his door, and knock. It takes him forever to come to the door. I keep knocking.

"What are you doing sitting on the floor?" He stands in the open doorway, barefoot, no shirt, wearing only a pair of jeans.

"I don't feel too good."

He takes my hand and helps me up. We go inside, and I sit on the only chair in the room.

"You got the flu?"

"No, Blake, I'm pretty sure I'm pregnant."

His face changes from a puffy-sleepy-pink to a tight shade of pasty white. He turns away from me, then back. His frown shows he's calculating his position. Like is he in for a paternity suit, or can he get a statutory rape charge on him? If he's picturing my dad in a bunny hood, it isn't funny anymore. I kinda feel like he wishes I'm not there at that moment. Then he softens and comes over to me and kneels down in front of my chair.

"You want a glass of water?"

"No, let me sit here for a while. I think it will pass."

He takes my hands, then feels my forehead. He stands up, goes over to the bedside table, and shakes a cigarette out of a pack.

"Why do you think you're pregnant? Could be the flu."

"No, this don't feel like the flu, and I think I might have screwed up."

"What do you mean, screwed up?"

He sits on the edge of the bed and lights the cigarette.

"I missed two pills."

"What? How could you miss pills? Don't you have one of those pill circles and a regular routine?"

"It happened before the dance recital. I got so wound up in it and was so nervous about my solo, I forgot. I know, it was a stupid thing to do, and when I realized it, I took extra pills to get back on schedule, but—put that out please, it's making me want to puke."

"Shit, Julia, this is fucked up." He stubs the cigarette out on the top of an empty soda can and sticks the dead butt in the can. "You can't be having a baby. Your parents will freak out. Are you sure you're pregnant because if you're messin' with me—I don't know what to do. What do you think we should do? I guess I could marry you..."

I laugh in spite of myself. Here I am, "mother with child" sitting on a chair in a one room apartment with an unemployed hippie father, whose sense of romance delivers a proposal of marriage with the words, "I guess I could marry you."

"No, Blake, you are not going to marry me. I am going to do the sensible thing a pregnant fifteen-year-old girl should do and that's to have an abortion. Don't worry. I'm not going to tell anyone, and nobody is going to hold you responsible. I'll make arrangements with the clinic and get it taken care of. But today, you need to do one thing for me—call the school, pretend you're my father and have them mark me off as sick for the day. I'm not going anywhere right now, and, if you don't mind, I think I need to lie down and take a little nap."

He helps me over to the bed, and I sleep until three that afternoon. I get up barely in time to catch the bus back home.

***

It's less than a week later that my parents recognize my boobs have begun to grow. It seems to happen overnight, and it becomes so obvious, there's no way to hide it. They ask me about it, and I tell them nothing is wrong—and it's none of their business. That doesn't go very far, and they try to get me to do a drug store pregnancy test which I fake. It's so easy.

INTERLUDE

STEVEN

Julia and I talked again after her Friday night dance class. She glowed with the physical joy of a good workout and success in execution of a difficult lift she'd been working on for weeks with her male partner. Now she wanted to bask in the feeling of accomplishment, and she needed someone to share it with. I was happy to be her audience.

We sat on the deck at the house with glasses of wine. The fresh smell of newly mowed hay surrounded us. The rhythmic clunk-ca-chunk of a bailer in the field below the house drew our attention. We watched it periodically issue string-tied hay cubes from its behind, like the droppings of a lumbering mechanical beast. The bales stood evenly spaced over the field. The low afternoon sun drew a long shadow next to each bale, creating a checkered geometric pattern on the trim grass field. The air was clear and cooling. I decided to take advantage of her good mood to bring up a difficult subject.

"Let's talk about the pregnancy, Julia."

"Oh, that," she said with a frown

"Remember when we made you take that drug store pregnancy test?"

"Oh yeah, that was stupid. I knew I was pregnant all right. I freaked out when mom tried to go into the bathroom with me. You must have known I faked the test."

"I knew, but there wasn't much I could do to make you do it right. When you came out of there with the false negative, we let it go. So here's the hard part, how did it feel to be pregnant?"

Julia picked up the bottle and filled our glasses. She held hers and looked out over the porch railing. I watched her shoulders rise and fall, then she turned back to me.

"It was awful. I was scared all the time and thinking about what I should do every minute of the day. I was afraid you'd send me back to the desert if I admitted it. I thought me and Blake could take care of it, and I wouldn't have to face you guys with it.

"For a while, I ignored it, told myself it wasn't happening. I didn't know for sure until my boobs started growing. Then I got mad at Blake for doin' it to me. Then Blake told me he would marry me, and I had that to deal with too. He would have done it, but I wasn't ready for that, and I didn't see a future with him anyway. Men are so impractical, boys are worse; it's a good thing women have some common sense."

"You made the right call that time, that's for sure. I can't imagine you having a child at fifteen and me having Blake around for the rest of my life."

"He wasn't that bad a guy, Dad."

"I'll let the judgment on that be determined some other day, OK?"

Promiscuous intentions
Not a lot of thought
Incongruous ambitions
Only fun was sought.
Reality ignored
Warnings not acknowledged
Authority over took it all
The barriers abolished.

Chapter 30

Steven

Mary confronted me, "She's pregnant. You have to do something. Since she won't admit it, or talk to us about it, we're going to have to find out some other way. She's on the phone talking to somebody every night. She must be telling somebody about it. It's not the kind of thing you don't talk about."

"I'll bug the phone." I said.

"You know how to do that?" Mary asked.

I did. I ran down to the electronics store and bought a recorder system. It had an automatic sensor that turned on a built-in cassette recorder whenever the phone line was active. I had run the phone wires to Julia's room when we did the remodel, so I knew exactly where the line ran in the crawl space under the house. I cut the wires and spliced in the recorder.

It took about a week. I would get the tape from the night before, and Mary would listen to it during the day when Julia and I were out of the house.

BLAKE: How are you feeling, Julia?

JULIA: I'm sick in the morning but I feel OK now. We have to do something, Blake. My parents know. They tried to get me to take a pregnancy test, but I faked it.

BLAKE:	I called the clinic. They won't talk to me. You're going to have to call. They said if you call, they'll get you right in for an exam.
JULIA *(Crying)*:	I don't know what to do. I can't have a baby. I'm fifteen years old. My life will be over.
BLAKE:	Please don't cry, Julia. It's going to be all right. I know other girls who've been to the clinic; it's not a big deal.
JULIA:	Oh yeah, how many girls have you sent there before me?
BLAKE:	Come'on, let's not be mean to each other. You aren't alone. We're in this together. I'm going to help you with this; it's only because they won't talk to me.
JULIA *(Crying)*:	Where can we get the money?
BLAKE:	I don't know how much it is, but I can borrow it from my uncle. He's cool, we can trust him.
JULIA *(Sniffling)*:	I'm tired, I have to sleep now. Please don't abandon me, I need you now.
BLAKE:	You know I won't. Let's go over to the clinic together tomorrow after you get out of school.
JULIA *(quiet)*:	OK, see you then.
BLAKE:	I love you.
JULIA:	I know.

By the fourth night we knew everything. The father was Blake, she was a couple months along, and they were planning to get an abortion. When we had all the proof we needed, Mary told me it was up to me to confront Julia. Mary went into the bedroom and closed the door.

I found Julia in the living room, picked up the remote, and clicked off the TV.

"Julia, we know you're pregnant. We want to help."

"I am not pregnant."

"We know you are planning to get an abortion, and we want to support you."

"I am not pregnant."

I started to yell at her. I was loud and in her face. "Julia, stop lying. We want to help you. When and where are you having the abortion? I'm going to be there."

The yelling got to her. Besides having the high emotions of a pregnant woman, she had never seen me like this. She shrank back into the couch and started to cry.

"Please don't send me away again," she sobbed, "I can't do that again. Please don't send me away."

I sat down next to her and toned it down.

"Julia, tell me when and where you are having the abortion. It is the right thing for you to do, but I want to be there for you. Tell me where and when."

That was when she lied to me. She gave me a date—wrong—and a place—wrong. I accepted what she said, but we kept working the phone tap and got the correct information in time.

***

When I walked into the clinic, I found Blake sitting there in the small waiting room looking glum. The little worm at least had enough honor to be there. He looked up at me with a blank face and turned away, like I was another problem added to the pile he was already dealing with, and "Oh well." I thought about confronting him, but then, what good would it do at this point?

I was immediately challenged by a clinic staff person who seemed concerned I might cause some trouble. I told him I was Julia's father, and he told me I had no right to be there—I told him I wasn't leaving without Julia. He wouldn't answer my questions or tell me where we were in the process, but Julia was out of sight so I assumed she was already inside. We had a little stare down until the guy backed away and went back behind their closed doors.

OK pal, I'm not going to try to enter your fucking inner sanctum.

We waited in silence. I had nothing to say to Blake. I was there for my daughter. He sat at one end of the room, me at the other. A half-hour went by, then another. Neither one of us picked up a magazine or said a word. We sat frozen in place with our thoughts.

Finally, a female nurse came out with Julia. She looked OK, physically. The nurse was tense. It was clear she didn't like my presence. Julia looked at me but didn't seem surprised to find me there. The nurse took a step to get between me and Julia, but Julia took her arm.

"It's OK," she said. Her voice was small, but it had a matter-of-fact, authoritative tone, like she expected everyone to know that she was in charge. The nurse eyed me warily but stopped.

"I'm here to take you home, Julia," I said as I stood up from my chair. I tried to voice a note of confidence I didn't feel. I held my breath, waiting for her response.

Julia looked at me, then at Blake. He got up from his chair, but she turned away from him. She dropped her head, time stopped, no one spoke. When she looked up, she turned to me, and a tear rolled down her cheek. She gave me her hand without a word. I felt the soft plea in her small fingers, the hand I'd held for so many years and I took her home to Mary.

ABOUT THE AUTHOR

Joseph Suste is an engineer, actor, playwright, fiction writer and poet. His short stories and social commentaries have been published in the Medford Mail Tribune and the Southern Oregon University school paper. He has been a radio announcer, performs in community theatre, and is active in a theatrical group acting-out poetry. He resides with his wife and daughters on a ten acre mini-ranch on the outskirts of Medford, Oregon.

AUTHOR'S NOTE

This story is a fiction with characters and scenes drawn strictly from the author's imagination.

The cover art was created by the author's daughter, Paige Suste, and the poems which preface some chapters are not his own but were chosen from several written by Paige and used with her permission.

After acknowledging that this story is a fiction, the author hopes the reader will find the writing is imbued with honest emotions that could be truly felt by a worried father and a maturing young woman.

The author is grateful to his beta readers, who have made valuable inputs to the manuscript. The members of Ruth Wire's Haywire Writers Workshop have been especially patient and helpful. Ruth Wire, Joshua Hendrickson, and Madeleine Sklar deserve my heartfelt gratitude. My sister Valerie Kavlick, Ruth Coppock, Theresa Ackerson, and Maria Ciamaichelo must also be recognized for their suggestions and careful edits. I am thankful to John Paul Owles of Joshua Tree Publishing, who smoothed out the wrinkles in the final manuscript and gave this book life.

For more information, visit:

JosephSuste.com